The silence in the truck was deafening.

"Want to talk about it?" he asked.

"I wish she'd wake up," Violet said. "Grandma's the key to all this." She fiddled with the fraying hem of her shorts. "I have a theory. Want to hear it?"

"Of course."

"I think Mary Alice said something that didn't sit well with Grandma, so Grandma started asking questions. I think whatever it was bothered her so much she couldn't just let it go or chalk it up to Mary Alice's confusion and nothing more. And I think it has something to do with Henry Davis."

Wyatt couldn't disagree. Violet's idea was as good as any he'd had, but hers worried him. If Violet was right, it would be dangerous for her grandma to wake up. Whoever had hurt her before would likely be back to finish the job.

Wyatt forced his eyes back on the road. Remembering his place in her presence was harder all the time. He was too attached. Too attracted.

DEADLY
COVER-UP

JULIE ANNE LINDSEY

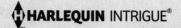

HARLEQUIN INTRIGUE®

Recycling programs
for this product may
not exist in your area.

ISBN-13: 978-1-335-13624-4

Deadly Cover-Up

Copyright © 2019 by Julie Anne Lindsey

This edition published by arrangement with Harlequin Books S.A.

For questions and comments about the quality of this book, please contact us at CustomerService@Harlequin.com.

® and TM are trademarks of Harlequin Enterprises Limited or its corporate affiliates. Trademarks indicated with ® are registered in the United States Patent and Trademark Office, the Canadian Intellectual Property Office and in other countries.

Printed in U.S.A.

Julie Anne Lindsey is a multigenre author who writes the stories that keep her up at night. She's a self-proclaimed nerd with a penchant for words and proclivity for fun. Julie lives in rural Ohio with her husband and three small children. Today she hopes to make someone smile. One day she plans to change the world. Julie is a member of International Thriller Writers and Sisters in Crime. Learn more about Julie Anne Lindsey at julieannelindsey.com.

Books by Julie Anne Lindsey

Harlequin Intrigue

Fortress Defense

Deadly Cover-Up

Garrett Valor

Shadow Point Deputy
Marked by the Marshal

Protectors of Cade County

Federal Agent Under Fire
The Sheriff's Secret

Visit the Author Profile page at Harlequin.com.

CAST OF CHARACTERS

Violet Ames—Single mother to an infant daughter, Maggie, returning to her childhood home following her grandmother's near-fatal accident. Strong and independent, Violet's previous involvement and subsequent abandonment by a military man has turned her away from men, especially military men. Until she meets Wyatt.

Wyatt Stone—Former army ranger and current cofounder of Fortress Security, a civilian protection agency. Wyatt was hired by Violet's grandmother days before her fall. He arrives too late to protect her, but vows to find her justice.

Maggie Ames—Violet's infant daughter, rocker of bonnets, thief of hearts.

Gladys Ames—Violet's maternal grandmother and surrogate mother. Faced with concerning information, Gladys hires Fortress Security to watch her back while she looks into the matter, but someone shuts her down before her protection can arrive.

Mary Alice Masterson—A dementia sufferer and lifelong friend of Violet's grandmother. She has recently begun to talk about people and events from her past that someone else clearly wants to keep buried.

Sheriff Masterson—Mary Alice's devoted son.

Sawyer Lance—Wyatt's former brother-in-arms and current partner at Fortress Security, arriving to provide backup and additional coverage while Wyatt and Violet search for the truth about what happened to her grandmother.

Mike Jones—A twentysomething serviceman gone missing and presumed dead more than forty years ago.

Chapter One

Violet Ames drove slowly along the familiar winding roads of River Gorge, Kentucky, wiping tears and saying prayers. It had been years since she'd visited the rural mountain town where her grandmother raised her, and this wasn't the return trip she'd planned. Her version had involved an abundance of hugs and triple servings of Grandma's double chocolate brownies, but there wouldn't be any of that tonight.

Violet divided her attention between the dark country road before her and the sleeping infant behind her. Eight-month-old Maggie dozed silently in her little rear-facing car seat, having given up tears to fatigue only moments after the car exited the hospital parking lot. Violet rubbed her heavy lids and tried to stay composed, but it had been a tough day.

According to the midmorning phone call she'd received from River Gorge General Hospital, Violet's grandma, a seventy-eight-year-old widow, had fallen from a ladder in her barn and nearly killed herself. The notion was unfathomable. Grandma's barn was old and left unused after her grandfather's death many years back, so why was her grandma even in there? And why had she climbed the ladder? There was nothing to reach with it except an old hayloft housing a decade of dust.

Violet gripped the aching muscles along the back of her neck and shoulders with one hand, steering carefully with the other. She couldn't get her mind around the awful day. "What would have possessed her?" she whispered into the warm summer air streaming through her barely cracked window.

That was a million-dollar question, because no one at the hospital had a clue.

Her grandma, the only one who could explain what on earth she'd been up to, was lying unconscious in a bleach- and bandage-scented room, worrying her granddaughter half to death. She'd undergone surgeries for her broken hip and wrist and received sutures on her cracked head and a wrap for her swollen ankle. What she hadn't done was open her eyes.

Her doctor said she'd wake when she was ready, and he had faith that would be soon. He'd suggested Violet be patient.

Patience wasn't Violet's strong suit. In fact, she wanted to scream. Her grandma had been Violet's entire world before Maggie was born, and she knew it. Violet had made her promise to be careful with herself the year she moved from River Gorge to Winchester, nearly two hours away. And she had. "Yet here we are," Violet muttered.

She thumped the steering wheel with one palm as hot tears spouted anew.

Maggie started behind her, jostling the car seat's

reflection in Violet's rearview. Violet couldn't see her face, but she heard the squirms and soft complaints as Maggie tried to find sleep once again.

Violet pressed her lips into a tight line, then wiped the new round of tears from her cheeks. They'd be at Grandma's house soon, where they could get a good night's sleep before returning to the hospital tomorrow, where hopefully they'd get some answers. Or better yet, find Grandma awake.

Soon the bumpy road grew steadily more uneven until cracked pavement gave way to sparse patches of dirt and loose gravel. Stones crunched and pinged beneath the tires and frame of Violet's little yellow hatchback as she maneuvered the final stretch to her former home.

A small smile pulled through her heartbreak as Grandma's farm came into view. Ghosts of her younger self on bicycles and horseback rushed down the drive to meet her, chased by the beloved hound dogs and yard chickens of her youth, sprayed with a garden hose held by her grandfather before he passed. Carried in Grandma's arms when her mother waved goodbye from the passenger seat of a station wagon driven by a man she barely knew.

Violet rolled to a stop in front of the old white farmhouse, nausea fisting in her gut and fat tears blurring away the world before her. She shifted into Park and climbed out to inhale the sticky night air. Summers in River Gorge were scorching hot with the constant threat of a thunderstorm. A volatile combination Violet had always loved.

She peered at her sleeping daughter. "This will be fine," she whispered. "Grandma will be fine." Unwilling to wake Maggie, Violet unlatched the entire car seat and hoisted it into her arms, baby and all.

With any luck, Grandma still kept a spare house key under the plant in the big red pot outside her dining room window.

Violet carried Maggie to the potted flower garden near the front steps and tipped the planter back with one foot. "Shoot." Nothing but bugs on the mulch-covered ground beneath.

She turned for the porch. All hope wasn't gone. Her grandpa used to keep a spare above the front door. Grandma had hated it because she was too short to reach without something to stand on. Violet, on the other hand, hadn't had that problem since middle school when she shot up to five foot eight and a half and stayed there.

She slowed on the steps when she caught sight of the front door already ajar.

Could the paramedics have forgotten to lock up on their way out?

Had they even gone inside the house if Grandma had fallen in the barn?

Violet flipped the interior light on and swung the door wide. Maybe her grandma hadn't fully secured the door before heading outside to the barn, and the open door had gone unnoticed by the EMTs.

Eerie silence greeted Violet as she edged her way inside, trying desperately not to wake her daughter. She set Maggie, in her car seat, against the far wall, then pushed the door shut behind them. "Hello?" she called, as much from habit and manners as anything.

The fine hairs along Violet's neck and arms rose to attention. The couch cushions were all slightly askew and a small drawer in the side table was open. She double-checked that the television and DVD player were still there, then shook her head in a relieved sigh. It wasn't a robbery.

Violet rubbed the gooseflesh from her arms. Of course it wasn't. No one in town would bother breaking into her grandma's house. For one thing, everyone was perpetually invited in, and for another, it was a small town. Folks here knew her grandma barely got by on her grandpa's small pension. Besides all that, there was nothing to take that Grandma wouldn't freely give.

A small sound rose on the night air, perking Violet's ears and causing her to rethink her theory. Another little bump drew Violet's attention to the kitchen near the back of the home and jerked her heart rate into a sprint.

She pulled her cell phone from one pocket and dialed the local authorities before inching away from the darkened hallway, back toward the front door and Maggie.

"Hello," she whispered to the tinny voice answering her call. "I think there's someone in my grandma's house."

No sooner had she uttered the words than a hulking shadow erupted from the home's depths, bearing down on her fast with long, pounding strides. Violet screamed as his iron hands connected with her shoul-

ders, knocking her end over end as he barreled past her
and out the front door.

Maggie screamed in her car seat as the calamity of
her mother's crashing body mixed with the loud bang
of Grandma's front door hitting the wall.

Violet scrambled onto her hands and knees, then
raced to Maggie's side. She climbed off the ground
slightly bruised but wholly motivated to get her baby
to safety. She wasted no time escaping the house with
Maggie and locking them both into her car, engine running, while she waited for local authorities to arrive.

WYATT STONE DOUBLE-CHECKED his GPS as the quiet
country road turned to gravel beneath his sturdy truck
tires. He knew Gladys Ames lived on a rural property, but this was nearly isolated. No wonder she had
been scared.

He drove with one hand on the wheel while he dug
through a pile of papers on his dashboard with the
other, fishing for a business card in decent condition.
Normally, Wyatt was better organized, but his fledg-
ling private security business had been growing legs
faster than he could keep up or recruit a staff large
enough to handle all the work, and that left Wyatt running on caffeine and determination more often than
sleep and preparation.

A set of bobbing headlights appeared around the
next pitted gravel bend and headed his way, demanding the lion's share of the narrow road and forcing
Wyatt's truck onto the grass with two wheels. The sheriff's cruiser lumbered past at a crawl, leaving Wyatt

to wait for the opportunity to forge on. Once he could, Wyatt pressed the gas pedal with a little more purpose than before. Gladys Ames had sent several messages to Fortress Security over the past few days, arranging for protection while she "handled some business," but Wyatt wasn't supposed to start work until tomorrow. So what had she gotten herself into that required a sheriff's presence since their last correspondence?

He slid his truck into the space behind a small yellow hatchback and climbed down from the cab.

A brunette with a baby in one arm and a half dozen assorted duffel bags dangling from her shoulders and hands froze at the sight of him.

It wasn't the first time a lone woman had looked at him that way. It wouldn't be the last.

His size and general appearance put most folks on edge, especially women. Certainly at night. Definitely alone.

Wyatt stopped moving.

"Ma'am." He tugged the curved brim of his worn-out Stetson and nodded. "I'm Wyatt Stone from Fortress Security, a private protection agency in Lexington. I'm here to see Gladys Ames."

This dark-haired beauty didn't speak or budge, though her arms must've been feeling the weight of her burdens. She was lean and tall for a woman, but Wyatt still had more than a half a foot on her. Like most people he met in this business, she looked incredibly vulnerable, breakable and scared. And he had a bad habit of looking dangerous, or so he'd been told.

Wyatt ran through a mental list of ways to get past

this beautiful guard dog without scaring her any further. He was there to help Gladys Ames, and a general web search had revealed her to be in her seventies. Definitely *not* this woman.

"I have a business card," he offered, "and a signed contract for services to begin tomorrow morning. I told Mrs. Ames I'd come sooner if I could. No additional charge, of course." Honestly, coming here straight from his last job had saved him five hours of traveling back to Lexington only to turn around and leave for River Gorge in the morning. He was going right past anyway. It made sense to start work a few hours early in exchange for an extra night of boarding.

The woman adjusted her baby on her hip and struggled with the cluster of bags hanging all over her. "Grandma hired you?"

"Yes, ma'am." Wyatt outstretched his hand, a new business card wedged between his fingers. "How about a trade? I take those bags off your hands, and you have a look at the card. Is Mrs. Ames inside?" He checked his watch, hadn't even thought about the time or a seventysomething woman's schedule. It was already after nine. "I don't want to wake her."

Tears sprang to the beauty's eyes and a small whimper puckered her rosebud mouth. "She's in the hospital."

Wyatt's senses went on alert. "Why?"

The woman slouched. Her face twisted in grief and agony. She made the proposed trade, then gathered her little girl more tightly against her chest, stroking her puffy brown curls.

Wyatt scanned the scene, impatiently waiting for

an answer to his question. Had someone hurt his new client before he'd even gotten there? The road-hogging cruiser came back to mind. "Why was the sheriff here?"

"Grandma's in the hospital because she fell. Sheriff Masterson was here because there was a break-in. He dusted for prints and took some photos of the mess, but nothing was missing as far as I can tell. He made a report and said he'd follow up."

Wyatt stifled a curse and headed for the house as eight years of military training and a lifetime of natural instinct snapped into effect. "How badly was Mrs. Ames hurt? Was anything taken? Who found her when she fell? I need as many details as you have."

He let himself inside and unloaded the bags onto a tweed couch beside the door. He ran his fingers along the jamb and door's edge looking for signs of forced entry, then did the same with the windows before moving on.

The condition of each room grew progressively worse as he pushed deeper into the home. The television was untouched, and a small dish near the kitchen sink held what looked like a set of wedding rings. "This wasn't a robbery."

He turned to discuss the situation further, but the brunette hadn't followed him inside.

Wyatt strode back through the house and onto the porch. "Are you coming in?"

"I don't know."

He shifted his weight and locked restless hands over both hips. "I'm not here to hurt you. I'm here to protect

Mrs. Ames, who assured me tomorrow morning was a fine time to start."

"Well, I guess she was wrong." The woman looked down at the card in her hand, as if she'd forgotten it was there.

"Tell me what happened." Wyatt moved to the porch's edge and lowered himself onto the top step. "I can't help until I know what I just walked into, but I assure you I *can* help."

Her eyes filled with tears again. "I don't know."

"You said she fell?" He highly doubted that was an accident, given her recent outreach to a security firm. "Is she going to be okay?"

"She's unconscious. Broke a hip and a wrist. She hasn't woken since the fall." The woman covered her mouth and nose with one trembling palm. A moment later, she stiffened her spine, wiped her nose and eyes against her arm, then locked both hands protectively around her daughter's back, seeming determined to be strong.

Wyatt pulled a handkerchief from his pocket. "Here."

"Thanks." She mopped her face and released a long, shuddered breath. "I'm her granddaughter, Violet, and this is my daughter, Maggie. I got the call this morning about her fall. We live in Winchester, so we came right out, and we were at the hospital all day, but she never woke up. I thought we'd stay here tonight, but when I got here…" She gave the house behind him a wary look.

Wyatt rested one boot on the step below him and

stretched his other leg out. He'd been in the truck far too long, folded up like a clean pair of fatigues. "I'm sorry about your grandma." He worked his jaw, considering the unusual set of events. "What do you know about the fall?"

"Not much, and what I've been told doesn't make sense." Violet rubbed one hand over her forehead. She'd clearly had a horrible day, and his unexpected appearance wasn't doing anything to improve it.

"Tell me what you do know."

She rolled wide blue eyes back to him. "The hospital staff said she was on a ladder in the barn, but Grandma hasn't kept anything in there in years."

Violet swung her face away from him and squinted into the darkness beyond the house. Her shoulders squared, and her expression turned suspicious and hard. The visible heartbreak was replaced by something Wyatt knew well. Resolve. "Maybe it's time we see the barn," she suggested.

Wyatt dragged his six-foot-four and two-hundred-fifty-pound frame back onto its feet with a nod of approval.

He and Violet were going to get along nicely.

Chapter Two

Wyatt moved alongside Violet toward the big red barn behind Mrs. Ames's home. He worked to keep his thoughts on important things, like what Mrs. Ames had been afraid of when she'd hired him, and not things like whether or not the wedding rings in the kitchen belonged to the intriguing brunette at his side.

Violet stopped at the back porch, standing with Maggie under a small cone of light thirty feet from the barn. She waved a hand in Wyatt's direction, indicating he should go on without her. The look on her face said the sleeping baby on her hip was Violet's priority. "There's a pull string just inside the door that'll give you some light. Not enough to fill the whole barn, but it's something."

Wyatt gave the ladies a long look before reluctantly leaving them behind. He'd already cleared the perimeter. He didn't sense anyone else nearby. They would be fine, and he wouldn't be long.

A few steps into the barn, a thin beaded-metal chain bounced against his forehead. He tugged it and squinted against the sudden burst of light. As promised,

it wasn't enough to explore the entirety of the cavernous structure, but it was all he needed. The ladder in
question stood just a few yards away, blood staining
the earthen floor at its base.

Wyatt accessed the flashlight app on his cell phone
and searched the ground more carefully, following a
line of blood to the small puddle a few inches from the
nearest ladder, making it obvious that someone had
wanted people to believe she'd been on the rickety-
looking structure when she fell, but that wasn't the
case. She'd fallen where the line of blood began and
had been moved to the ladder, where she continued
to bleed until someone had found her. Aside from the
blood trail, the dusty ground had been heavily trod-
den for an unused barn, probably evidence of whoever
had discovered her and the emergency team who had
taken her away.

"Do you see this?" he asked softly. His senses
pinged like rapid fire. Violet's nearness charged the
air between them. He didn't need to look to know she
was there.

Violet gasped, then shuffled closer, having given up
her hiding spot around the corner. "How'd you know
I was here?"

"It's my job." And he had a feeling he'd sense her
anywhere now that they'd met. Never mind the fact
that the sweet scent of her so easily knotted his chest
and scrambled his thoughts.

Training had surely played a part in his ability to
track her movement without looking her way, but never
in his life had he been so acutely aware of any woman,

or so distracted by the question of where she placed her perfume. Did she dab it on her wrists, the curve of her neck? Along the valley between her breasts?

"Impressive," she said, sounding as if she meant it.

Wyatt had always been astute, but the army had honed his natural talents to a lethal point. Those skills had been incredibly useful as a soldier but were an unyielding burden as a civilian. Hearing every sound. Knowing every lie. Those were the reasons he'd rarely been at ease since his return stateside and the catalyst for opening his private security firm. That and the fact that he was good at what he did, maybe even the best. Wyatt read people, and he protected them.

Currently, Violet seemed to be deciding if she could trust him. The answer was a resounding yes, and he'd prove that to her with time. The shifting glances she slid between him and the open barn door suggested she was also wondering whether or not she could out-run him.

She could not.

Wyatt lowered the beam of his light to the stained floor. "Who found her?"

"Ruth," Violet said. "A friend of hers I ran into at the hospital. Grandma had invited her for lunch, but didn't answer the door, so Ruth looked out here and saw the barn door open."

Wyatt considered the new information. "Mrs. Ames broke her hip and wrist? Did she receive any injury that might have resulted in this kind of blood loss?"

Violet's skin went pale. "She hit her head. They gave her a bunch of stitches." Her free hand traveled absently to the crown of her long wavy hair, as if she might feel the sutures there.

A head injury explained the blood.

Wyatt extinguished the light and tucked his phone back into his pocket. "If your grandma was on the ladder when she fell, how do you suppose she hit her head only a few inches away from the base?"

Violet's brows knit together. Her attention dropped back to the shadow-covered floor. "She couldn't have."

"Right. With her body on the ladder, her head would've hit farther away, unless she fell headfirst from the loft, which would've done more than break her hip and wrist." He pulled his father's Stetson from his head and rubbed exhausted fingers over short-cropped hair. "I think she fell over there." He pointed to the wide start of a narrow line of blood, then swung his finger toward the ladder. "Someone moved her closer to the ladder, probably hoping whoever found her would jump to conclusions, which they did."

"So she didn't fall off the ladder."

"I don't think so, no."

Violet's beautiful face knotted. Her blue eyes snapped up to lock on his as recognition registered. "Grandma hired you because she thought she needed protection."

"Yes, ma'am."

"From who?"

He placed the beloved hat back onto his head. "She didn't say."

Violet's dark brows tented. "Do you think whoever it was might have done this to her?"

"That's what I intend to find out."

VIOLET WATCHED AS Wyatt grabbed the aged wood of the barn ladder and gave it a shake before climbing into the old loft. She'd never met anyone as big as Wyatt and watching him climb the ladder conjured memories of the giant on Jack's beanstalk. Her grandma was wise to choose him. If anyone could protect her, this would be the guy. Everything about him screamed military training. She recognized his rigid stance and searching gaze. She'd seen similar traits in Maggie's father, though the caution and compassion in Wyatt's voice had never been present with her ex. Violet's heart panged with regret at the unbidden memories rushing to the surface. She'd been naive to trust her heart so easily, and look where that had gotten her.

Maggie wriggled and Violet kissed her soft brown curls. She lifted a hand to shield her sleeping face from another round of dust falling from the loft. At least she'd gotten Maggie from the carnage of her train wreck relationship. Awful as the love loss had been at the time, she'd gladly endure it again if that meant she'd get to be Maggie's mama.

Violet stepped away from the growing cloud of rustled dirt floating in the air. Soft scents of aged wood and dried hay slipped into her senses, sending a flood of nostalgia over Violet's anxious limbs. "I used to spend hours in that loft," she said, letting her voice carry to Wyatt. "Grandpa died when I was in middle school, and Grandma sold the animals, but I still came out here." Trying to feel near him.

The creaking boards went silent. Wyatt had stopped to listen. "What was up here then?"

"Just hay and me."

"What did you do?"

She smiled at the massive Wyatt-shaped shadow on the wall. He must've gotten his cell phone light out again. "Read. I was going to be a pilot like Amelia Earhart, or a Nobel Prize–winner like Marie Curie. Maybe a scientist like Jane Goodall." Violet had bored her grandma to death recounting all the things she'd learned up there.

"Are you?" Wyatt's deep tenor voice carried through the quiet air.

Violet chuckled, bouncing Maggie gently against her chest. "What? A pilot or Nobel Prize–winner or scientist? No. I'm a fifth-grade language arts teacher." As it turned out, Violet enjoyed telling others the things she knew more than she wanted to go off and do them herself. She only wished her grandpa had lived to see her with her class, sharing the stories he'd loved with them. He would've been so proud. And he would have loved Maggie.

Wyatt's steady footfall moved back toward the ladder. "There's a good-sized bare spot up here. Looks like either something pretty big was kept here or someone was clearing a spot for some reason."

"How would anything get up there?" That was the whole conundrum, wasn't it? "Grandma couldn't carry anything up a ladder, especially something large." And they'd already established that she hadn't fallen from the ladder. She'd probably never even been on it.

Wyatt's long legs swung into view, and he returned to her side by way of the creaky rungs. "Take a look."

He brushed his hands against his thighs, then turned his camera to face her. A picture of the dispersed hay overhead centered the screen.

"It looks like someone was just kicking it around to me," Violet said. "The whole floor is dusty. The space would be cleaner if something had been there long."

Wyatt rubbed the back of his neck, then the thick black stubble over his cheeks. "You're right. I should've seen that." He pressed his fingertips against heavy-lidded eyes. "I know you've had an awful day, and you're still deciding what to think of me, but can I trouble you for some coffee? I've got enough work to keep me busy a while, and I've been on the road all day."

Violet pulled her gaze to the open barn door and back. She'd checked out Wyatt's company website on her cell phone, using the business card he'd given her, while she'd waited briefly outside. Under the tab with details about the protectors for hire, she'd found photos of Wyatt. Posing in his dress greens. Running drills in fatigues. He seemed to be who he said he was. One founder of a private protection firm in Lexington. "What kind of work do you have to do tonight?"

He dropped his hands to his sides, then stuffed long fingers into the front pockets of his jeans. "I didn't see any signs of forced entry inside the home, so I'd like to replace the locks and dead bolts for starters, install motion lights at the front and back of the house, and add chains on the main entries."

"You're doing all that tonight?" Violet squeaked. Did he think that whoever had broken in and knocked her down might come back? A shiver coursed over her and she held Maggie tighter.

"Basic precautions," he said. "I've got everything I need in my truck, and a copy of your grandma's contract if you want to see it. Given the circumstances, I think she'd allow that."

Suddenly, the stranger before her seemed like the safer, handsomer of two unknowns. Violet was certain she'd sleep better with new locks and a trained military man under her roof. Besides, it was after ten already, and Maggie never slept past six. If Violet didn't get to bed soon, she wouldn't get much sleep.

Wyatt ducked his head. "I don't mind sleeping in my truck and starting tomorrow if that makes you more comfortable." He moved toward the string for the light and slowed for Violet to pass. "You've been through a lot today, and I've slept in that truck more often than my bed this month. I'd still like to get the new locks on first." His cheek ticked up in a lazy half smile before he shut it down.

Violet stopped to face him. She chewed her lip in indecision. "Why did Grandma choose you?"

"I'm the best."

Violet made a show of rolling her eyes, silently thankful for his efforts at levity given the day she'd had. "Humble, too."

Wyatt pulled the light string, delivering them into darkness as they made their way back outside. "I advertised strategically. Specifically to women's groups, yoga studios, churches that had events likely to be attended by elderly civilians. Word spread like wildfire. I suppose she found me that way."

Violet narrowed her eyes. "So you targeted women and old folks."

He nodded confidently. "Statistically they're the most common targets for violent crimes, harassment and stalking. I wanted to make a difference, not play bodyguard for some rich jerks."

Violet mulled the answer, impressed yet again. "You were planning to stay with Grandma while you're in River Gorge?"

"That was the agreement," he said. Wyatt matched his pace to hers as they walked back across the lawn to Grandma's home. "I have a week blocked off on my calendar for this, but I can stay longer if something changes. Mrs. Ames only said she had something to take care of, and she wanted the freedom to do it without having to watch over her shoulder." He grinned, sneaking a quick look in Violet's direction. "I was going to be her nephew, visiting from Lexington."

Violet rubbed the creases she felt gathering on her forehead. That cover story made Wyatt her relative, and it didn't say much about her, given the things she'd already thought about him. Like how nice he might look without a shirt. Or pants.

She turned her heated cheeks away.

It wasn't like her grandma to meddle, so Violet could only assume that whatever was going on had been dropped into her lap. *And it must be something big to force Grandma's involvement and require a bodyguard.*

She slowed at the front porch and turned to face Wyatt. "Will you be able to find out if her fall was an accident?"

"Yes."

"And if it wasn't, will you find out who hurt her?"

He dipped his chin in sharp confirmation. "I won't leave town till I do."

Violet evaluated the giant before her. He certainly seemed legit, and her grandma had chosen him. She'd even trusted him to stay with her while she did whatever it was that she was doing. "Okay," she said, resting her cheek on top of Maggie's head. "You can stay, and you don't need to sleep in your truck." She marched up the steps before she changed her mind. "I'll make up the couch and put on the coffee."

They went their separate ways then. Wyatt to his truck for his bags. Violet to set up a portable crib for Maggie in her grandmother's bedroom. She returned a few minutes later with a baby monitor and bedding to cover the couch.

Wyatt was already hard at work changing door locks in the kitchen. "I wouldn't have blamed you if you didn't let me in tonight," he said, attention fixed on the open door and his work.

"I wouldn't have cared," she said with a smile. If she'd suspected he was a danger to Maggie, his feelings would have been the least of her concerns.

Wyatt released a low chuckle. "Fair enough."

She started the coffee, then stuck a mug under the drip. "Cream or sugar?"

He shook his head in the negative. "Just the caffeine."

"Right." She carried the cup of coffee to her handsome handyman, then turned in a small circle, deciding where to begin remedying the mess left by an intruder.

She started with shutting cupboards and drawers, then moved on to clearing the counters. "What do you think Grandma was looking into that made her so afraid that she called you?"

"Well." Wyatt shut the back door and tested the locks before tossing a set of identical keys onto the counter and unearthing a chain system from his bag. "Could be anything." He lined the chain's casing against the door's edge and cast a look in her direction. "Did she say anything unusual to you lately?"

Heat crept over Violet's cheeks as she struggled to recall the last time she'd spoken to her grandma. "We don't talk as much as we used to. I've been busy since Maggie was born."

"How old is your baby?"

Violet chewed her bottom lip, debating how much to tell him about her life "Eight months. She didn't sleep for the first four, but she seems to be making up for it now."

He smiled.

"I can't complain. Even single moms need a break sometime, right?"

Wyatt's sharp brown eyes snapped in her direction. His gaze drifted to her left hand, then rose to her eyes. "Not married?"

"No. Never. How about you?" she asked. "Any children? Got a Mrs. Stone at home?"

"No, ma'am."

"Why not?" The words were out before she'd thought better of them. Then again, maybe this was the smart move. If he'd openly admit his inevitable defects, then she'd stop imagining the snare of electricity coursing between them at every turn. The fact that they were virtual strangers should have been enough to keep her from wondering what his hands might feel like on her hips or in her hair, but it hadn't. Maybe knowing he was a womanizer, gambling addict or married to his job would do the trick.

"I hear I'm a pain in the ass," he said, making the final few twists of his screwdriver. "Apparently, I'm cynical, distrusting and tenacious to a fault."

Violet laughed. "Comes with the job, I'd suppose."

"You're not joking." He slid the chain into the slot and tested the door. "I make my brothers crazy, and I've guarded their lives in combat. If they can't handle me, I'm not sure why anyone else would want to try."

Violet swept a pile of broken glass onto a dustpan and transported it into the trash. "How many brothers do you have? Any sisters?"

"No siblings." Wyatt frowned over his shoulder. "Sorry. I meant my brothers-in-arms. Sometimes I forget they aren't my blood, but we are undeniably family. Sawyer, Jack, Cade and I formed Fortress Security about two years after my military discharge. We've all tried to fit back into our civilian lives, but it didn't work for us. We're too far changed, and our particular skill sets don't translate well to civilian life." Wyatt packed up his tools, jaw clenched. "Eventually I decided to open a business where we could do what we've been trained to do. Guard and protect."

Violet's stomach tilted at the mention of his military service. "What branch did you serve in?" Maggie's dad was a marine.

"US Army Rangers." He seemed to stand impossibly taller as he reported the information. "Sawyer and Jack were, too. We met at Fort Benning." Pride puffed his chest and deepened his voice.

Violet found herself drifting closer, hungry to know more. "A security firm run by army rangers? Also impressive."

"It would be," he said, smiling, "but Sawyer's brother, Cade, was a jarhead."

Violet's mouth went dry. She didn't mean to judge an entire branch of the US military by the actions of one pregnant-girlfriend-abandoning creep, but the association was there nonetheless, roiling in her gut.

"We've all got our mottoes and taglines," Wyatt said, "but the bottom line for Fortress Security is honor first every time. Doesn't matter how you word it."

"God. Corps. Country. Family," Violet groused.

"Exactly."

Exactly. Violet set her broom aside and went to see what she could clean in the dining room.

Wyatt Stone might be kind, sexy and undeniably charming, but that marine motto had pulled her back to reality. The truth was that men like Wyatt would always put family last.

And that would never be good enough for Maggie.

Chapter Three

Violet woke on a gasp of air. Her heart caught in her throat as the faceless monster of her dreams vanished with the warmth of morning sunshine drifting through her grandma's bedroom window. The beloved scent of her childhood was everywhere, on the pillows and sheets, in the curtains and carpet. She took a long steadying breath of the floral dime-store perfume before peering over the bed's edge into her daughter's portable crib.

Maggie grinned around a mouthful of her toes, drool running down her chubby cheek. She released her foot instantly, reaching tiny dimpled fists greedily toward her mama.

Violet scooped her daughter into her arms and rolled back onto the antique sleigh bed for a long snuggle. "Today will be a better day," she promised. "We'll go see Grandma, and the doctors will say good things, and soon we'll be having breakfast with her instead of the enormous cowboy sleeping on the couch."

Maggie laughed and slapped Violet's cheek with one slobbery hand.

Ten minutes later, the Ames ladies were dressed in jean shorts and tank tops, prepared for another hot July day. Violet left her hair down, curling over her shoulders to her ribs, instead of pulled coolly into a ponytail. She told herself it wasn't for Wyatt's sake despite the already rising temperatures.

There was something about the way he'd turned those knowing brown eyes on her last night. The way he'd watched and listened to her, seeming to perceive everything, as if he could read her mind.

Given the handful of inappropriate things she'd fallen asleep thinking about, all starring him, she was thankful to be wrong about the mind reading.

Violet braced her shoulder against the curved wooden headboard and put her weight into shoving the bed away from the door. Barricading the room seemed silly by the light of day, but she wasn't exactly the best judge of men and inviting one the size of Wyatt to sleep over had seemed questionable after she'd come upstairs.

Doorway clear, Violet popped Maggie into a baby sling and headed silently downstairs to start breakfast without waking Wyatt. Six fifteen was early for anyone. It had to be an unthinkable hour for someone who had needed caffeine to stay awake at ten last night.

The beloved scent of fresh-brewed coffee met her in the stairwell as she descended into the kitchen, and Violet hurried toward it. Could Wyatt be awake already? And have had time to make coffee?

His bare back came into view a moment later, and she stopped to appreciate the way his low-slung basketball shorts gripped his trim waist, accentuating his ridiculously broad shoulders and thick, muscular arms.

"Hungry?" he asked without a single look in her direction. It was the second time he'd seemed to magically know she was there.

Violet moved casually into the kitchen, pretending not to have been ogling him. "I thought you'd be asleep."

Wyatt shuffled scrambled eggs around one of her grandma's iron pans and smiled over his shoulder. "I like to run before dawn. Watch the sun rise. Clear my head for a new day."

Violet gave a small laugh. "You've already been out for a run?" The only thing she liked to do before dawn was sleep.

"Sure. A run. A shower. Breakfast. I brought some aerial photos of your grandma's land with me in case I needed them this week, so I used them as guides and went around the property's edge. It worked nicely because I didn't want to go far from here without letting you know I'd be out. I wasn't sure when Maggie would wake."

Violet worked to shut her mouth. He remembered Maggie's name? She'd only introduced her once, and her baby had been asleep the whole time.

"Mrs. Ames has a nice setup here," he said. "Nearly fifty acres. Some of it is being farmed on the back side. Looks like she rents that to a local farmer. Everything near the house is incredibly peaceful, and there's a beautiful lake past the rose gardens."

Violet nodded. The rose gardens were her grandma's

pride and joy. She raised blue-ribbon winners almost every year. The lake had always been Violet's favorite outdoor spot, especially in the summer. There was a nice breeze under the willows and when that didn't keep her cool, the shaded waters of the lake did.

Wyatt flicked the knob on Grandma's stove to Off. He shoved rich, buttery-scented eggs onto a plate and ushered them to the kitchen table, already set for two. "I helped myself to the fridge." A grimace worked over his face. "I hope that's okay. I plan to replace everything I used when I go into town. Just thought you'd be ready to eat once you woke."

Violet blinked. "Thank you."

He returned to the stove and levered fat strips of bacon from a second bubbling pan, then layered them on an oblong plate heavy with napkins to soak up the grease. "I grew up on a farm like this. Ours was a horse farm, but this place reminds me an awful lot of home."

"Good times?" she guessed by the wistful look on his face.

"Every. Single. Day." He tossed a red checkered towel over one shoulder and delivered the bacon to the table.

Violet's gaze traveled over his perfect chest to the jaw-dropping eight-pack abs below. A dusting of dark hair began beneath his belly button and vanished unfairly into his waistband.

"Oh." He looked down at himself. "Sorry. Bad habits." Wyatt disappeared into the next room and returned in a clingy black T-shirt. "Eat up. Big day."

Violet tried to hide her disappointment at the change

of scenery and discreetly checked for drool. "What's on the agenda?" she asked, settling Maggie into the legless high chair clinging to the kitchen table's edge.

"I'm headed into town," Wyatt said, taking a seat beside Maggie with his loaded plate.

Violet turned for the counter and prepped a bottle of formula, then dug through her diaper bag for Maggie's favorite yellow container of Cheerios. "Breakfast is served," she said, delivering the pair to Maggie. Violet lifted her eyes to Wyatt. "What's happening in town?"

"I'm going to talk to folks," he said. "See what they have to say about your grandma and anything else that might be turning the rumor mill." He sipped his coffee and smiled at Maggie.

She threw a Cheerio at him and missed by a mile.

Violet went to pour a cup of coffee. Clearly, Maggie could hold her own.

Maggie's squeal of delight spun Violet on her toes.

Wyatt bit into a slice of bacon, utterly straight-faced while her daughter clapped and laughed.

"What are you doing?" Violet asked, enjoying the rush of pleasure at seeing her baby smile.

Wyatt chewed and swallowed slowly. "What?"

"Maggie squealed."

Wyatt glanced innocently at the pudgy-cheeked princess. "She did?"

Violet narrowed her eyes in a ruse of disapproval. "You know she did. You're sitting right beside her." She dropped her gaze to pull out a chair, and Maggie cracked up again. This time, Violet caught sight of Wyatt's pink tongue sticking out sideways before he pulled it back in. "Did you just make a face at my baby?"

"No, ma'am."

"I saw you make a face at her," Violet insisted, trying hard not to smile around the edge of her coffee mug. "You lied to me."

Wyatt slid serious brown eyes toward Maggie. "Snitch."

Maggie rocked and bebopped in her seat, eyes fixed tightly on Wyatt.

He wiped his mouth and set the napkin on the table beside his already-empty plate. "Okay. Truth? I've made several faces at your daughter this morning."

Maggie blew raspberries until spit bubbles piled on her chin.

"Oh!" Violet giggled. "Maggie!" She wiped her baby's chin and let the laughter grow. "I've never seen her do that before." A tear slid from the corner of one eye as she dotted Maggie's nose with the napkin. "What a nut."

Wyatt winked at Maggie before turning back to Violet. "What are your plans today? Do you want to join me in town before we visit Mrs. Ames, or would you rather see her first, then head into town afterward?"

The words were innocent enough, but they itched and scratched at Violet's heart and mind. She'd known Wyatt less than a day and suddenly it seemed as if they were playing house. *When were they visiting Grandma? When were they going into town?* They. Violet, Maggie *and* Wyatt.

She took a moment to absorb the scene around her.

A handsome, attentive man had made her breakfast. He'd made her daughter laugh, and he'd unwittingly made Violet think of things that were impossible. Like a cute little nuclear family of her own. She felt so incredibly stupid. The connection she imagined between herself and Wyatt obviously boiled down to him being the first man who was kind to her following Maggie's birth and nothing more. He was simply being professional. He was there to do a job, not fulfill Violet's fantasies. And she needed to get a grip.

Violet pressed a hand discreetly to her tummy, quashing leftover butterflies. "No. Thank you." She couldn't allow herself to think impossible things. It wasn't fair to her or Maggie. And what was wrong with her anyway? Since when was she so eager to have a man in her life? Things were good already. "I think we'll visit Grandma on our own," she said. "You can do what you need to do, and we'll catch up with you later."

Violet pushed onto her feet and carried her still-full mug and plate to the sink. With her back securely facing the table, she squeezed her eyes shut and pulled herself together. Lots of people made babies laugh. Wyatt wasn't the first or the last, and she couldn't get attached to him because of it. Much as she wanted a traditional family for Maggie, the kind with a mommy and a daddy who kissed goodbye and held hands while they watched TV, Wyatt wasn't that guy.

She opened her eyes and straightened her expression before turning back to the duo making goofy faces at the table. "We should probably get going."

Wyatt tipped his head in that unsettling way, the one

that made her feel as if he could see straight through her. "You sure you don't want me to come with you?"

"Yep." She pushed nervous fingers into the back pockets of her shorts. "We're fine, and we don't want to keep you from your work. The sooner we know what really happened to Grandma, the better. If she's awake when we get to the hospital, I'll call you so you can come by and talk with her in person."

His thick black brows knit together. "All right."

Violet pulled Maggie into her arms and posed her on one hip, then gathered her bottle and Cheerios in the other hand. "Have a good day."

VOICES OF HAPPY children rang through the speakers inside Violet's little yellow hatchback. The CD of nursery rhymes lightened her heavy mood as she fought through a fresh bout of worry for her grandma.

Sunlight streamed over the hills to her left, dashing the street in shards of amber and gold light. Puffy white clouds sailed in the brilliant blue dome above. It was a perfect day for a drive, and Violet had desperately needed to clear her head.

Putting some distance between herself and the sexy soldier guarding Grandma's home was just a bonus. She recalled seeing him pull up in his big black truck, check out the house and shuffle through papers on his dashboard. When he'd climbed out and stood as tall as a house, complete with cowboy hat and boots, her heart had given an irresponsible thud.

"Dumb," she muttered, taking another look at the

rear-facing car seat in back. Maggie didn't need a daddy any more than Violet needed a boyfriend *or husband*.

The two of them were doing just fine on their own.

She smiled and returned her eyes to the road ahead. Flyers for the county fair waved and rippled on passing telephone poles, stapled beside missing pet posters and garage sale signs.

A half heartbeat later, her thoughts swept back to the shirtless man making her breakfast. Surely *that* wasn't part of his contract.

The gentle hum of an approaching engine edged into Violet's thoughts, erasing the memory of Wyatt seated beside Maggie at the breakfast table. The sound grew steadily louder, and Violet searched in every direction for the source of the aggressive hum.

Her little hatchback hugged the next curve, dropping low over a hill and into a valley just two miles from the county hospital. She forced her attention back to the road, but her roaming eyes returned to the rearview mirror with a snap.

A battered blue-and-white demolition derby car roared earsplittingly into view behind her as she crested the next hill.

Maggie's car seat rocked in frustration.

"Thanks a lot," Violet muttered at the mangled car racing closer in her rearview. She removed her foot from the gas to let the lunatic pass before they reached the next uphill curve and crashed. Violet's current speed was nearly fifty in a forty-five, and the sharp sway ahead was marked as fifteen miles per hour.

The wrecked car revved closer with an ominous growl. This time, the driver laid on the horn.

Beep!

The seemingly endless blast sent Violet's heart rate into a sprint. She stuck her hand out the window and waved the guy to go around.

He didn't.

Instead, the attacking car roared closer until its entire front end was invisible in her mirror. *Beeeep! Beeeep!*

Maggie stirred, then began to wail at the continued horn blasts and growling engine.

Violet returned her foot to the gas pedal, pressing a little harder than necessary in an effort to put space between the other vehicle and herself. "Sh-sh-sh," she hushed Maggie, hoping to return her to a gentle sleep.

Maybe she could drive the speed limit as far as the next turnoff, then get away from the road-rager behind her. Or maybe he'd just pass her and move on when she used her signal.

Violet sipped oxygen and concentrated on the narrow two-lane road ahead.

The offending car dropped back a few inches, then charged forward once more, its hood half disappearing in the rearview.

Violet pressed the gas pedal and prayed.

Her death grip on the steering wheel grew painful as her little hatchback floated over the asphalt with a psychopath on its tail. Her fingers were snow-white and sore from lack of circulation.

The fifteen-mile-per-hour curve was coming up

fast, and Violet was losing faith in her plan. She had to be able to slow down to take the next turn or pull over, but the beast behind her wouldn't allow it. She realized with a punch of fear through her chest that this could be the end. She could wreck her car with Maggie strapped helplessly in the back seat. The idea was almost too much for her to bear.

Maggie's desperate wails echoed through Violet's heart and ricocheted off the walls of her racing mind until her vision blurred with fear and regret. They were trapped.

Beep!

Violet watched in horror as the assailing car dropped back, then lurched forward one last time. The reduced-speed sign flew past them, and Violet jerked her wheel.

Her little hatchback careered off the side of the road moments before reaching the steep bend and went skidding through the grass and gravel of a tiny church lawn and empty parking lot.

Beside them, the little white church stood alone at the base of the perilous curve.

The demolition derby car barreled onward, flying into the curve at high speeds and squealing its tires and brakes for several long seconds before the dreaded engine noise faded into the distance.

Violet pulled her keys from the ignition, then climbed out on shaky legs and unlatched Maggie from her car seat. Together, they moved to the church steps and sat, embracing and crying for so long Violet thought someone might find them and wonder if she'd lost her mind.

Maybe she had.

Frighteningly, she and Maggie had nearly lost so much more.

Chapter Four

Wyatt strode back into the blazing midday sun, adjusting his worn-out Stetson and squinting against the light. A trip to the local bar had proven equally as useless as all his other stops today. Wyatt had ordered a sweet tea for the sake of manners, then asked the motley lineup at the bar what they knew about Mrs. Ames. They'd all pointedly ignored him. Though it had been Wyatt's experience that small-town folks were occasionally tight-lipped when it came to outsiders, he'd usually had great luck with the men drinking their way through daylight. Local bars were the male equivalent of a beauty parlor for gossip and hearsay. Except not here. The handful of men who had bellied up to a beer and a shot glass at this bar had officially broken the mold. And just like the local diner, hardware store, mechanic and barber, no one had any news to share about Mrs. Ames.

Wyatt took his leave of yet another uncooperative group and headed back onto the street. He spun his key ring around one finger and took a long look in both directions. Where to next?

A sheriff's cruiser slid against the curb before he'd had time to decide. The cruiser's lights flashed. No siren. The man who climbed out was nearing fifty with narrow shoulders and a shiny star on his chest.

Wyatt tipped his hat and stepped aside, allowing the local sheriff room to pass on the narrow sidewalk. The town was a modern-day Rockwell portrait waiting to happen. So what had brought the sheriff and his flashers out? Wyatt paused, waiting to see where the local lawman would go. Had there been another "accident" like Mrs. Ames's? Or perhaps the bar patrons had reanimated and grown rowdy in Wyatt's absence.

The sheriff stopped in front of Wyatt and rested a palm on the butt of his sidearm. "Are you the stranger going door-to-door and making folks nervous?"

Wyatt glanced over his shoulder in search of a shady, bothersome guy.

No one was behind him. The sheriff was definitely talking to Wyatt.

"I don't think so, sir," Wyatt said. "I've been out enjoying your lovely town. Meeting folks. That's all."

The sheriff gave a long, assessing look. "Where did you come from?"

"Lexington," Wyatt answered, this time returning the scrutiny. Irritated, he crossed his arms and widened his stance. "You been sheriff long?"

"Long enough."

Wyatt smiled. "Someone reported me for being friendly?" He'd love to know who, but didn't have to ask to know the sheriff wasn't telling. Too bad, because whoever had made the complaint might also be the one with something to hide. A recent B and E for example, or maybe an assault on an old lady. "Is that a crime in this town?" Wyatt had spoken to a dozen locals, but he'd been careful not to ask anything too pointed. He'd asked if anyone knew Mrs. Ames, if they'd heard about her fall, and where he might get a good locksmith after the break-in. He'd already changed the locks, of course, but he'd hoped to read folks' expressions. See who was shocked by the news of a burglary and who already knew. Problem was that no one had paid any attention to him at all.

The sheriff sucked his teeth and grimaced. His stance was rigid, defiant, not at all welcoming or pleasantly confident. Wyatt pegged him for a bully. "What business brings you to River Gorge?"

"I'm visiting."

"Who?"

Wyatt homed in on the sheriff's features, the beating pulse in his throat, the dilation of his pupils. "Gladys Ames. Do you know her?"

The sheriff nodded. "I know everyone, but I've never seen you. Are you a relative?"

"No. Mrs. Ames is my girlfriend's grandma," he improvised. "I came to watch over her while she's here. Seems there was a break-in last night. You were there, right?" Hadn't Violet said it was a Sheriff Masterson whose cruiser had forced his truck into the grass on the narrow gravel road? "Got any idea who would've done something like that?"

A pinch of guilt tugged in his mind for announcing Violet as his girlfriend, but Wyatt wasn't about to tell the sheriff who he really was or why he'd come to River Gorge. Not considering the inquisition he was getting just for speaking to locals. For all Wyatt knew, the sheriff could be the reason Mrs. Ames needed his help in the first place. She certainly could have chosen to talk to the sheriff instead. And if he was being honest, the idea of being Violet's boyfriend wasn't a bad one. Which was confusing all by itself, because Wyatt didn't do relationships.

Sheriff Masterson cocked his hip. "Funny. Violet didn't say anything about a boyfriend when I spoke to her last night. She surely didn't mention anything about a man coming here to stay with her."

"Can you blame me? She was attacked inside her grandma's home. I couldn't stay away after that. Turns out I'm the overprotective sort." He straightened to his full height and locked his jaw, an intentional reminder that Sheriff Masterson might have the star, but Wyatt was there to protect Violet and Maggie. Anyone with different plans would have to go through him, and no one ever had. "Any leads on the break-in? Seems strange, doesn't it? Someone busts into an old lady's house, tears it up but takes nothing. She lives on a widow's pension. What was there to take? And the crime occurred on the same day she allegedly fell from a ladder." Wyatt furrowed his brow. "As the sheriff, that must send up some red flags."

"Crime happens everywhere. I'm looking into the break-in, but old ladies fall all the time." He gave Wyatt a more thorough look then, trailing him head to toe, lingering on his jacket, sides and ankles. Looking for

signs of a weapon? If he had anything to say about
the gun nestled against his back, or knife in his boot,
Wyatt had a permit to carry concealed firearms and
more training than the good sheriff could fathom for
the knife. "Military?" he asked.

"Ranger."

The sheriff nodded; a rueful smile budded on his
lips. "Violet know about that?" He snorted, clearly
laughing at Wyatt. For his service? For his doomed
pretend relationship?

Wyatt bristled.

A pair of women in fitted running gear came into
view behind the sheriff, having rounded the corner
from the direction of the local park. The taller, blonder
one locked eyes with Wyatt. A coy smile curled the
corner of her mouth. The petite redhead followed suit
a moment later.

Wyatt smiled back.

Sheriff Masterson turned on his shiny shoes to follow Wyatt's gaze. He tapped the brim of his hat and
smiled at the women. "Afternoon Maisey, Jenna."

The ladies slowed to a stop, still smiling at Wyatt.
The blonde outright ogled him. Her hand bobbed up
for a shake. "Jenna Jones," she said. "I don't believe
we've met."

"Nice to meet you," Wyatt answered, taking her
thin hand in his. "I was just asking the sheriff if he'd
heard anything new about Mrs. Ames. She fell yesterday, then her house was broken into."

"No," the ladies gasped.

The blonde, Jenna, stepped closer, still holding his

hand. "Mrs. Ames is the sweetest woman. I've known her all my life. Is she okay? I didn't hear about the fall."

The redhead looked at the sheriff. "Did he say someone broke into her house? Why would anyone do that? Do you have a suspect?"

Wyatt rocked back on his heels. Apparently his usual stops were all wrong in River Gorge. Normally, men spoke easily to him. Wyatt would break the ice on topics like sports, cars and military, then ask the things he really wanted to know. Around here that hadn't been the case. Maybe he should've simply gone jogging.

Jenna joined her friend then, turning to stare at the sheriff. "Are you going to answer her?" The tone was harsh and familiar. Wyatt doubted Jenna was related to the man; more likely they'd been former lovers or shared another form of history. Either way, she looked like she'd like to punch his face, and he looked like it wouldn't surprise him if she tried.

The sheriff sniffed. "I'm looking into it."

"Well, when you're done with that," she said, "maybe you could spend some time patrolling our streets. We just watched a demolition derby car run a hatchback right off the road by Devil's Curve. When are you going to do something about the morons using the county route as some kind of playground for their stupidity?"

Wyatt's heart seemed to stop. "What kind of hatchback?"

"Small," the redhead said. "Yellow, I think."

Wyatt's feet were in motion, pulling him away from the trio and toward his truck parked down the street.

He turned to jog backward, needing to know but also needing to go. "Was anyone hurt?" He freed his phone and dialed Violet while he waited for the answer.

"I don't think so," Jenna said. "The car spun into the church parking lot, but it didn't roll and it wasn't hit. The beat-up old junker went sailing around the curve. A woman got out. She looked fine. We were on the towpath. It wasn't easy to see from there, but all the honking and engine roaring had gotten our attention. We caught the tail end of it all."

Wyatt's limbs ached to run. "When?"

"Maybe an hour ago."

"Thank you," he called, turning and diving into a sprint. The call connected and rang against his ear. *Pick up. Pick up. Pick up.* He willed Violet to answer his call. Prayed she and her infant daughter were okay. Kicked himself internally for letting her go off on her own when everything in him had said it wasn't safe. That whatever Mrs. Ames had gotten herself into wasn't over. He should have followed Violet, stuck by her, protected her.

It wouldn't happen again.

He yanked the driver's-side door open and swung himself behind the wheel. *Pick up.* He nearly screamed the words as he shifted into Drive and eased away from the curb.

His call went to voicemail.

VIOLET FORCED HER still-rubbery legs forward as she eased off the hospital elevator and down the long white corridor toward the nurse's station on her grandma's floor. Maggie was asleep in her arms, exhausted from crying after their run-in with a lunatic and his demolition derby car. The nurses were all busy when she finally arrived at the desk. Talking to visitors. Speaking on the telephone. Making rounds. None of the ladies in pastel scrubs made eye contact. When Violet had arrived yesterday, her cousin Tanya was one of the nurses. She was a distant cousin, ambiguously related, but neither she nor Tanya had ever questioned the connection. They'd been friends all their lives. Violet waited a long moment, scanning the area for an available nurse, before moving on, too eager to continue waiting. She wanted to see her grandma's face and take a seat someplace where she couldn't be run off the road. She'd try the desk again in a few minutes when the rush died down.

Violet hurried down the hallway to her grandmother's room. The sound of movement inside set Violet's heart alight. "Grandma?" She rushed through the open door and slid the curtain back with bated breath.

"Hello," her grandma's friend Ruth answered, "come on in." Ruth tidied her stack of playing cards, then cut and folded them together with a scissoring zip. She'd pulled a chair over to face Grandma's bed and appeared to be playing solitaire on her blankets. "No change," Ruth reported. Her tanned cheeks were spotted from too many decades in the sun, and her lips turned down at the corners, unhappy with her report. She doled out three cards and placed them near the foot of her bed. "I came after my morning chores." Her hair was pulled back in a severe bun, accentuating her sharp features and small green eyes.

Violet took the chair nearest Grandma's shoulder and slid one hand over hers where it rested on the bed. Machines glowed and beeped on stands and poles nearby, monitoring her grandma's heart rate, pulse and oxygen levels. An IV dripped something into her veins. A wave of grief rolled through Violet and she forced the emotion down. Grandma wasn't gone. Grandma was a fighter. "Has the doctor been in?"

"Just Tanya," Ruth said. "She comes every hour or so to say nothing's changed." Ruth gave the cards a break and hooked one ankle over her opposite knee. A lifetime of hard outdoor work in River Gorge had left Ruth roughly the color of leather and likely a little tougher. "No news is good news."

Violet didn't agree. No news was maddening. She shifted Maggie in her arms and squeezed her grandma's hand. "Tanya was here yesterday when we got in from Winchester."

Ruth pursed her lips. "She's a good kid."

A twist of guilt wound through Violet. She and Tanya were the same age, twenty-six. Hardly kids. But Violet hadn't been here for Grandma. She'd left for college, and unlike Tanya, Violet hadn't come back. In fact, she'd visited less and less these last two or three years. She should have at least stayed the night at the hospital, shouldn't she? She rested her cheek against Maggie's head. No. She couldn't have stayed. She'd spent last night half fearing a second break-in and half curious about what the cowboy-for-hire on Grandma's couch might've done to anyone who'd try.

Her throat tightened at the memory of the fleeing intruder. He'd run straight for her. Broad palms plowing into her shoulders. He'd thrown her onto her backside in the space of a heartbeat. She'd found bruises on her back and elbows when she showered. Marks from where she'd crashed against the hard floors and rolled. Twelve hours later, a car had run her off the road. There was no way that was a coincidence. Even Violet's luck wasn't that bad. Her gaze ran back to her grandma's bandaged head. A near-fatal fall, a break-in, a psychotic road-rager, the hiring of a private security guy. That list definitely added up to something, and it wasn't coincidence. In fact, Violet needed to contact the local sheriff's department and make a report about the demolition derby car. Even if the driver wasn't found, it seemed like a good idea to document the strange and dangerous things happening around her. She'd considered calling the police from the church parking lot, but she and Maggie were too shaken, and the offending car was long gone. All she'd really wanted was to find respite somewhere with witnesses in case the car returned. Could the car's driver be the same man who'd been inside her grandma's home?

"Ruth," Violet began, turning back to Grandma's friend. "When you found Grandma yesterday, was the front door open to her home? Ajar maybe?"

"No." Ruth shook her head as if to underline the word. "I knocked. Rang the bell. Door was shut tight. Why?"

"Did you go inside?"

"Sure," she said. "Wasn't locked. Rarely is. I let myself in and took a look around. I called for her, but she wasn't there. I figured she'd run out to the garden to cut some roses, so I went around back. That was when I saw the barn was open."

"That's when you found her," Violet said.

"Yes." Ruth blinked emotion-filled eyes. "That's right."

"Do you have any idea why she was in the barn? Was she keeping something out there?"

"Not that I know of." Ruth raised a wide gray eyebrow. "Why?" She twisted in her seat to face Violet, a strangely parental look in her eyes. "Why all these questions? Did something else happen?"

Violet slumped in her chair, unsure how much she could say. It was impossible to know her limits without knowing what her grandma had been up to, but she was certain Ruth was a friend. Ruth had been part of Grandma's life long before Violet was born. Before Violet's mother, too. "Her home was broken into last night."

"What?" Ruth gasped. "Are you okay? Is the home? What did they take?"

Violet shrugged. "I don't know. Nothing seemed to be missing, but I haven't been here in a while." Honestly, she'd barely been anywhere since Maggie was born. These last eight months had boiled down to meeting her baby's needs and trying to calculate how many hours of sleep she might get each night. The answer to the second part was "never enough."

"A break-in," Ruth whispered, still clearly baffled.

"How has Grandma seemed to you lately?" Violet asked. "Was she okay, or was something going on with her?" Violet tipped slightly forward, begging Ruth to share something that might help her understand.

Ruth puckered her brow and stared at Grandma's slack face. "She's been a little on edge and distracted. I'd assumed that had to do with Mary Alice."

"What's wrong with Mary Alice?" Violet asked. She knew Mary Alice as well as she knew Ruth. Both women had been lifelong friends of Grandma's. They'd held Grandma together when her daughter, Violet's mom, had left, when her husband passed, and when she'd had to raise a grieving, rebellious granddaughter despite it all. "Is she…" Violet began, then halted. "Is Mary Alice…" She came up short again. Was there a nice way to ask if an old woman had died?

Ruth scrutinized Violet's struggle for words. "Mary Alice isn't dead, if that's what you were going to ask," she said after a few seconds. "She's got dementia, though. The symptoms have gotten a lot worse these last few weeks. She's slipping away fast, and the whole Masterson family has been a little grouchier than usual these days. The illness has taken a toll on everyone close to her, your grandma included."

Violet didn't know Mary Alice's family well, aside from the general knowledge small town living provided. Her husband had been the sheriff when Violet was young, and their son was sheriff now. Neither man was in the running for Mr. Congeniality, or the sort who'd show up at local gatherings, unless duty demanded it. "And you?" Violet asked.

Ruth gave a sad smile. "Someone's got to hold it together."

Tanya peeked her head through Grandma's open door and rapped her knuckles on the wall. "Knock knock." Her bright smile set Violet on her feet.

"Tanya." She met her cousin at the room's center and gave her a gentle hug, careful not to wake Maggie. "Any news?"

"Not yet," she said, rubbing Violet's arm when she stepped out of the embrace. "Dr. Shay says everything looks good, and we should be patient. Grandma will wake when she's ready. Until then, we just have to wait. She's been through a lot and it can take time to overcome an accident like this one. How are you and this little princess holding up?"

Violet stroked Maggie's back and her sleeping baby released a contented sigh. "We're okay."

"Good." Tanya smiled. "I'll be here as often as I can, and I'll keep you posted if her condition changes. Grandma's tough, Violet," she assured. "She'll be fine."

Violet nodded. Grandma would find the strength to recover, and Violet would be there to help every step of the way. Until then, Violet needed to stick a little closer to the former ranger at Grandma's house. Violet had no intention of testing her luck with another burglar or demolition derby car, and she was certain he would have no problems handling either.

Of course, spending too much time with an attentive and sexy man like Wyatt Stone was going to pose a few problems of its own. Beginning with how to keep her undeniable attraction to him from blurring the lines of their reality.

Chapter Five

An engine roared outside the front window of Grandma's home. Violet jumped, still edgy from her run-in with the demolition derby car this morning. She'd called the police as soon as she got home and the woman who'd answered had promised to send an officer out to take the report, but she doubted any of the deputies would be racing to get to her.

Her heart sprinted and her palms grew slick as she moved carefully toward the front window to check the driveway. Maggie was asleep in her crib, but Violet could get to her and be outside in under a minute if she had to. She pulled the curtain's corner back with trembling fingertips, scolding herself once more for not taking Wyatt's suggestion to stick together today.

Relief washed through her chest at the sight of Wyatt's truck, back in the driveway. He was already making his way up the front steps in long, anxious strides.

Fresh terror rent Violet's heart as she took in his grim expression. Whatever had drawn that kind of fear on Wyatt's face was surely something for her to worry about. "Wyatt?" she asked, opening the door with an anxious tug. "What's wrong?"

His steps faltered a moment as his eyes landed on hers. "You're okay," he said, sounding half awed and half stricken. "Someone said a car fitting your vehicle's description was run off the road this morning. I thought for sure it was you. I tried calling. You didn't answer." His exacting gaze lingered on her face, her neck, her chest. "You're frightened. Breathing hard. Your cheeks are flushed. It was you, wasn't it?"

Emotion swept up from her core, taking her by surprise. "I called the police, then I worried that the car's driver would somehow know I tattled and come revving up the street looking for me. It's ridiculous. I know. I'm sorry I didn't answer."

"You need to save my number. When I call, I need you to answer."

Violet nodded. "Of course. I will next time."

"Did you get a look at the driver or the license plate?"

"No plate, and I couldn't see the driver through the tint and glare. It was crazy, though. He came out of nowhere," she said, hating the tremor in her voice. "He kept honking. Gunning his engine. Maggie was screaming."

Wyatt stepped closer and raised one tentative arm, an offering of comfort, hers to accept or deny. Violet hesitated. She didn't want to cry on a near-stranger's shoulder, but she needed the comfort, and she'd never see Wyatt again once this was over. So maybe she could be a little bit of a mess if she needed to be.

She fell against the strength of his chiseled chest and wrapped her arms around his back. His heart pounded strong and steady beneath her ear. His clothes and skin smelled of cologne and body wash, and Violet inhaled deeply.

A very long moment later, his arms circled her back, engulfing her, drawing her close in a powerful embrace. "It's okay," he said. "You're okay."

She rocked her cheek against his soft black T-shirt. "Thank you. For being here. For coming to help Grandma and for staying now. I don't know what I would do here alone. I don't know if it's safe to stay, or if it's safer to go. If I leave, what happens to Grandma? If I stay, what might happen to Maggie?"

Wyatt curved his tall frame over her, lowering his mouth to her cheek. "I will protect you, your grandma and your daughter. You can trust me on that, and when I find out who is behind these violent acts, he will wish I hadn't."

Violet shivered. The words were flat and controlled, not spoken in anger, just statements of fact and strangely horrifying. Still, she wanted the promise to be true. "Thank you."

The bark of a police siren jerked her upright. She loosened her grip on him as she attempted to disentangle her arms from his waist.

Wyatt held her firm, locking his fingers against the small of her back. "I told the sheriff we were a couple," he whispered. "We shouldn't ruin the facade."

Violet tipped back, arching to study his blank soldier face and pressing their torsos tighter still. "What? Why?" Was that something he'd actually considered?

"He had a lot of questions," Wyatt said. "I ran into him in town, and I didn't want to out myself as private security."

"Right." She nodded. This wasn't about her. He simply needed a cover story. He didn't want to be her boyfriend. That was a fantasy she'd already let go too far. Besides, she knew firsthand that when men swept in to save the day, they were always gone in the morning. And Violet didn't need drama in her life. She needed stability.

The deputy marched in their direction, one hand at the brim of his hat. "Miss Ames?"

"Yes." Violet stepped away from Wyatt. She wrapped an arm across her middle, defending against the coolness that settled in his absence. She shook the deputy's hand. "This is Wyatt Stone, my boyfriend." She cleared her throat as the last word lodged there awkwardly.

Wyatt took the man's hand smoothly and with confidence, as if it was no big deal for her to announce herself as his girlfriend and suggest all that the title might imply.

"I'm Deputy Santos," the man said, looking the couple over. "I'm here to make a report." His olive skin was the perfect accent to his shaggy jet-black hair and deep ebony eyes. "Were you both in the car when the incident occurred?" he asked Violet.

"No," Violet said. "It was just my baby and me."

Deputy Santos removed a small flip notebook from his shirt pocket and turned to an empty page. "Can you tell me everything you remember about the car, the driver and the incident?"

"Sure. I mean, it's not much, but I'll try," she said.

The deputy took notes as she described the incident from start to finish in as much detail as possible. His gaze rose from the paper when she described the car that had chased her.

Wyatt shifted his stance. "You know that car?"

The deputy returned his attention to the paper, finishing whatever he'd been in the middle of writing. "I can't say for sure, but I will look into it." He tapped the tip of his pen against the paper. "Anything else?"

Violet shook her head. "No. That's it." Something about the deputy put Violet on edge. He was hard like Wyatt, without the pretense of friendship.

He nodded, then turned to Wyatt. His gaze dropped briefly to the india ink tattoo stretching from beneath his shirt sleeve. "You serve?"

Wyatt dipped his chin sharply. "Ranger. You?"

Deputy Santos stood straighter. His stern expression eased. "I was Delta Force once upon a time."

Wyatt smiled. "It's nice to meet you." A strange vibe cropped up between the men. "Can I ask you something?"

Santos narrowed his eyes, cautious again. "You can ask."

"Did the sheriff's department get a call this afternoon about a man talking to folks downtown?"

The deputy's brow wrinkled in confusion. "About a man talking to people? What do you mean?"

Wyatt shook his head. "Nothing. Let me ask you something else. How well do you know the sheriff?"

Santos blew out a long breath. "Not well." He crossed his arms and widened his stance, seeming to consider whatever he would say next. "I got into law enforcement after the military. I came to River Gorge a few years back because I needed work, and this department had an opening. It didn't take long to see the Mastersons run this town. And that's fine. I don't want to run the town. I just do my job and skip the company picnics."

Wyatt bobbed his head. "Fair enough."

The deputy gave Violet a long look, then turned for the driveway. "The report will be available online tomorrow. First copy is free from the secretary at the station." He pried the door of his cruiser open and dropped behind the wheel. A moment later, he was gone.

Maggie's cries erupted through the baby monitor in the living room.

"Sounds like dinnertime," Violet sighed, checking her watch.

Wyatt opened the front door and held it for her to pass.

"Maggie's like a little hobbit, eating every meal twice." Lately, Violet couldn't seem to stomach more than coffee. She hoped Maggie's continued interest in food was a sign that she wasn't as stressed out as her mom.

"Hey." Wyatt reached the interior steps before Violet. "Why don't I get Maggie, and you can start her dinner? Teamwork. Yeah?"

Teamwork? Well, that was a new one for Violet, especially in terms of childcare, though she absolutely wasn't opposed. "Okay. Thank you." Reluctantly, she headed for the kitchen, attention focused on the cries still registering through the baby monitor.

"What are you doing?" Wyatt's voice boomed from the little speaker in mock breathlessness.

Maggie hiccuped, then gave a shorter, softer complaint.

Wyatt groaned. "You're so heavy. I can barely lift you. Oh my goodness." He panted.

Violet smiled as she prepped Maggie's bottle and chose a jar of peas with carrots for her baby's midafternoon snack.

Maggie giggled, then complained, more softly still.

"Okay," Wyatt agreed. "I'll try again, but you have to help me."

"No!" Maggie yelled the only word she'd perfected.

Wyatt gasped. "What?"

Violet stifled a bubbling laugh. Maggie was every kind of cute, but Violet could already tell she was going to be a real pistol.

A moment of silence passed, then he laughed. "You didn't tell me you could talk. What else can you say?"

"No!" Maggie growled, then laughed.

"Wow." Wyatt's quick footsteps rocked down the stairs a moment later, and he had Maggie in his arms. "I don't mean to be critical, but your baby's kind of negative."

"No!" Maggie stated as if on cue.

Violet laughed. "That's her only word. Be nice."

Wyatt placed her in the high chair and put his hands on his hips. "You probably should teach her something else. What if someone comes by here offering a million dollars or free ponies?"

"No," Maggie answered, then squealed, utterly thrilled with herself.

Wyatt lifted one palm and shoulder as if to say she'd made his case.

Violet delivered Maggie's bottle and bowl of baby food with a smile. She took a seat at Maggie's side and began to spoon the veggies up.

Wyatt poured two glasses of iced tea and brought them back to the table with him, setting one before Violet and sipping the other. "I ran into the sheriff today."

"Yeah?" Violet lifted her gaze to him. "You asked the deputy about a call to the department. Was that true? Someone called the sheriff on you?"

Wyatt stretched his neck. "I don't think so, but that was what he claimed when he found me."

"Huh," she huffed, frowning as she stirred the pureed food. "He seemed fine when we spoke last night after the break-in."

"Do you know him very well?" Wyatt asked. "You grew up in River Gorge, right?"

"Yeah, but I don't know him well," she said, spooning another bite into Maggie's open mouth. "Grandma and I never had any reason to need the sheriff. I know his mother, but not him. Honestly, I hadn't had reason to speak with any of the local lawmen before today."

Wyatt set his tea aside, considering her words. "The sheriff seemed to know you."

"How so?" Curiosity flamed in her mind. "Did he say something?" Violet could only imagine the things the sheriff might have heard secondhand through the local grapevine, especially after Grandma and her friends returned from Violet's baby shower last year. Violet had still been reeling from the sting of rejection and fear of impending motherhood, and she had been less than gracious when asked about the baby's father.

"He seemed to imply you don't like military men." Wyatt shifted his gaze to Maggie. "Her father served?"

Violet stiffened. "Yes."

"Was the sheriff right?" Wyatt asked. "You have something against military men?"

Violet dropped the little spoon, then scrambled to pick it up, hating the anger and humiliation the thought of her ex brought her. "Sheriff Masterson doesn't know anything about me." She exhaled. She didn't want to talk about Maggie's father, but avoiding the topic would only make her look more pathetic. Might as well get the story out and over with, not that there was much to tell. "Maggie's dad was a marine," she said. "I thought we were in love, and he shipped out making big promises about our future. We had a bit of a whirlwind romance, so I can blame myself for that." She shot Wyatt a sheepish look. Whirlwind romances weren't something Violet normally participated in. She tried to be much more levelheaded than that, but her ex had been so persuasive, so charming. "We traded emails for a while, but after I found out about the pregnancy, he disengaged. Completely. Changed his number. Stopped returning emails. Maybe closed the account. I don't know, but I gave him every opportunity to know her, to be part of her life, even if I wanted to strangle him for breaking my heart. He wasn't interested."

Wyatt appraised her with those careful dark eyes. "I'm sorry," he said eventually.

"My heart was stupid, and I won't let it happen again." She offered an apologetic smile. She always felt guilty for speaking poorly about Maggie's dad, even if he was a big jerk for what he'd done. "At least I got Maggie out of the mess. I don't know what I'd do without her."

Wyatt made a sour face at her baby. "I don't know. She's pretty negative."

Maggie formed a wide toothless smile. "No."

Violet laughed as she wiped carrots off Maggie's sticky cheeks. "Are you sure this isn't just your natural effect on women?"

A deep belly laugh broke free from Wyatt's lips; it bounced in his chest and reached his eyes. "No. I'm honestly not sure at all." He turned the captivating expression on Violet and silence settled over the room.

"I'm glad you're here," she said. "And I don't have anything against military men. I'm thankful for each of you and for your service."

He watched her carefully, as if he was expecting something more.

Violet offered a handshake. "I'm glad to know you, Wyatt Stone."

He folded her hand in his. "It was my honor."

Their joined hands stilled. He'd held on too long

and she'd let him. What did that mean? What would
he think it meant? Violet pulled away, busying herself
with clearing the high chair tray.

She didn't have to have something against Wyatt
to keep her heart on guard. They could be friends.
Work together. Help her grandma and then part ways.
Nothing more. She rubbed her hands roughly against
a kitchen towel, trying not to enjoy the way he spoke
sweetly to Maggie at the table or the way she blew
him kisses off the palms of her chubby dimpled hands.
No. This wasn't permanent. Not even semipermanent.
This was a flickering moment in her life, already on
its way past.

WYATT FOLLOWED VIOLET off the back porch and into the
sun. She'd said she needed some fresh air, and he couldn't
bring himself to let her go alone. Not the way things were
going down around her in this town. She'd tucked her
baby into a circle of fabric and hung her off one hip like
a purse. It was the weirdest thing Wyatt had ever seen
someone do with a baby, but Maggie appeared happy.
She kicked her bare feet and looked eagerly around. Violet kept a protective arm around her, but thanks to the
construction of the sling, he thought, remembering what
Violet had called it, Violet's hands were both free, too.

Violet stopped to admire her grandma's roses. Little
stone plaques placed among the mulch identified the
various bushes as county prizewinners. Wyatt didn't
know much about flowers, but he could understand
why these beautifully manicured plants had gotten so
much glory.

"I think Deputy Santos knew that demolition derby car," Violet said, squinting against the sweltering sun. "There was recognition on his face at the mention of it, and how many cars like that one can possibly be in one small town?"

"Maybe," Wyatt agreed. He'd seen the look on Santos, too, but he had to be careful about assuming it meant anything more than surprise. "He seemed like an honest guy. He might make a good ally. After my run-in with the sheriff today, I'm sure he's got something against me, and he's the head honcho here. If he wants me arrested for interfering in his investigation, I'm going to jail. And I can't help you from there."

Violet paused, turning to face him. "So, he doesn't report to anyone? That's a lot of power in a little county like ours."

"It's a lot of power anywhere," Wyatt said. He shook his head. "Maybe my brothers are right when they say I'm cynical."

"Well," Violet said, "I think a little cynicism is warranted here. Something is definitely wrong. Someone hurt Grandma, broke into her home and ran me off the road. Then the sheriff said he got a complaint about you in town, but the deputy didn't hear about it. Makes me wonder if someone's holding something over the sheriff, maybe even keeping him from acting on valid threats and feeding him information on bogus ones. I think there's a good reason Grandma called you and not local authorities."

Wyatt rubbed his chin, struggling to stick with the facts at hand. "There could be a number of reasons she came to me instead. Maybe she felt she couldn't trust anyone here to keep her confidence, even the sheriff. In small towns, most people are connected somehow. News spreads. Could be that she needed more than a cop to watch her back. If she felt she was truly in danger, it's not as if a local deputy could move in with her temporarily. And I got the feeling, through her emails, that she might've wanted a little help looking into something because she asked about the agency's ability to research."

Violet played with Maggie's little hands as they walked, her gaze on the horizon, brow furrowed in thought. "Did you say my grandma wrote you emails? Did you keep them? Can I see them?"

"Sure."

Violet turned on her toes and headed back to the house.

Wyatt followed. "Are you getting hungry? You didn't eat anything earlier. There's plenty of vegetables in the garden, and I saw a grill on the rear porch."

Violet shot a skeptical look over her shoulder as she opened the side door to her grandmother's home. "You don't have to do any of that."

"I don't mind." The words came easily, congenially, and Wyatt realized he meant them. He liked the idea of cooking for Violet. "Here." They stopped in the kitchen, and he swiped through the emails on his phone before presenting the device to her. "These are all the emails I received from your grandma."

"Thanks." She set Maggie on the floor and handed her a large plastic block with a bell inside. "Okay."

She accepted the phone then, lips moving slightly as she read the messages to herself, scrolling slowly. "I hate that she was afraid and didn't call me," she said. "I don't know what I could have done, but I wish I would've known. I feel so helpless."

Wyatt pressed a palm to her back, rubbing a small circle before pulling his hand away. He stuffed the offending fingers into his pocket. Violet wasn't his to touch. She was a client's granddaughter, and in a few days the mystery would be solved. She'd be back in Winchester, and he'd be in Lexington trying to forget the beautiful, smart and kind brunette who'd gotten under his skin from hello.

"Wyatt?" Violet turned to him, a strange expression on her face.

"What?"

"Grandma doesn't have a computer. So how'd she send these messages?"

The sudden roar of a massive engine split the afternoon air, stopping him from taking a guess. Glass shattered outside, and his truck alarm raged in response.

Wyatt raced to the living room and opened the front door. His truck lights flashed in protest at the apparent assault.

On the lane, a set of taillights fishtailed away, attached to the rear end of a blue-and-white demolition derby car.

Chapter Six

Violet dialed the police again, wishing she could put in a request for which officer would respond this time. Wyatt seemed to trust Deputy Santos, but she was leery of everyone today. She definitely hadn't liked talking to Sheriff Masterson on the night Grandma's house was broken into. He'd treated her with tamped-down hostility even then. Now she pressed her back against the front wall and peered outside. She watched as Wyatt stormed down the drive, then up the road a few yards in the direction the taillights had disappeared.

Maggie tugged on her leg, trying and failing to pull herself upright.

She scooped her baby into a hug and covered her in kisses.

"Violet," Wyatt's voice boomed through the window.

Violet jumped.

Outside, Wyatt stood, hands on hips, in the driveway. He'd shut the blaring truck alarm down, and was scowling at her little hatchback parked in front of his pickup. "You can come out," he said a little softer, though still loud enough to be heard from inside the home.

She opened the door slowly, then moved across the threshold as Wyatt lifted a cell phone to his ear. Maggie fussed on her hip, eager to be put down as Violet drifted to Wyatt's side on autopilot. He asked someone on the other end of his call to send a deputy back to his location.

Two police reports in one day.

In the quietest town on earth.

The sun heated Violet's skin, and the scent of prize-winning roses wafted on the breeze. The nostalgia was thick, but this wasn't the town she remembered.

The passenger window of Wyatt's truck was shattered. Shards of glass glittered on the drive in tiny chunks.

"Hopefully Santos is back here in a few minutes," Wyatt said, stuffing the phone into his pocket. "He can add this to our growing list of assaults. It might make him look a little more closely at the people in his town." Wyatt's hard brown eyes swept from her face to the vehicles. "I'm sorry you got the worst of it."

Violet followed his gaze to her hatchback. Her stomach dropped as the damage to her little car registered. Six jagged letters were scratched into the paint of her driver's side. *GO HOME.* "Oh my goodness." Her heart hammered and her throat thickened. The letters stretched from wheel to wheel. It was impossible to misinterpret the instructions.

GO HOME.

It was an order. It was a threat.

Who would do this? Why?

Wyatt wrapped one strong arm across Violet's back and pulled her and Maggie against the hard-muscled vee of his side. He rubbed her arm with his palm, creating heat where goose bumps had risen despite the sweltering temperatures. "You can have it repainted."

She pressed a hand to her mouth, then nearly jumped out of her skin when the *whoop!* of a deputy's cruiser bleated behind her, already pulling into the drive.

Wyatt squeezed her a little tighter. "Great," he muttered.

Violet turned for a look at the new arrival. Not Santos, and not a deputy's cruiser.

It was the sheriff.

WYATT BRISTLED AS Sheriff Masterson climbed from his cruiser and moseyed serenely to their side, glancing only briefly at the damage to their vehicles.

"What seems to be the trouble?" he asked.

Violet made a strangled sound beneath the hand on her lips.

Wyatt tightened his fingers on her biceps, reassuring her he had this. "You got here awfully quick, Sheriff. I've barely disconnected my call to dispatch."

The sheriff's gaze drifted then, from Wyatt to Violet and Maggie. "I was in the neighborhood."

"Yeah?" Wyatt's voice deepened. He felt his muscles tightening to spring as he leveled a no-nonsense stare on the cocky lawman. "Any particular reason for that? Mrs. Ames's place isn't exactly on the beaten path."

"Seems you two need all kinds of help these days,"

he said, giving the vandalized vehicles a pointed look. "I figured I should keep an eye out."

"And yet you missed the culprit by only a few minutes." Wyatt rubbed his chin. "You probably got a good look at the car, though, since you were in the neighborhood. A blue-and-white demolition derby car." He raised his brows. "Sound familiar? It went hightailing out of here not ten minutes ago."

"Nope." The sheriff rocked on his heels and stuffed his hands into his pockets. "I didn't see anything on my way over except this pretty day."

Violet shifted, and Wyatt dropped his arm from around her, unwilling to hold her there if she wanted to go inside. Instead, she rolled toward him, burying her face and hands against his chest, pressing Maggie to him with her. Wyatt's arms curled around them on instinct, making promises of protection he couldn't yet voice.

The sheriff took a few steps closer to the vehicles. "You certainly are having a lot of problems here. I'll make the report on this, but you've got to admit it begs a couple questions."

"Such as?" Wyatt pulled in deep breaths of clean country air and forced his temper into check.

"For starters," the sheriff said, moving past them to kick the front tire of Violet's car, "who'd you upset enough to do something like this? And why?" He squatted before the damage and dragged a finger along the deep lines. "Also gotta ask why you don't just take the advice here and go home." He creaked back onto his feet and shook his head. "Seems like the best way to protect that baby of yours is just get away from all this mess."

Violet tensed. She spun to face the sheriff. "Are you suggesting my baby is in danger? That the man who ran me off the road and vandalized my car might attack my infant? Is that what you're saying?" There was fire in her voice as she pulled her body away from Wyatt's, no longer afraid, no longer wanting protection. It was Violet's turn, her instinct, to defend what was hers.

Wyatt smiled at the sheriff.

The sheriff raised his palms. "No one said that."

"You implied it," she snapped. "And I don't like it. I'm staying here to see that my grandmother recovers from her fall. While I'm in River Gorge, I don't expect to be harassed and threatened. I expect you, the sheriff, to see to it that I'm not. Otherwise, what is your job exactly?"

Sheriff Masterson blinked long and slow. The fatheaded smirk fell from his lips.

Wyatt covered a laugh with a cough. He couldn't afford to lash out the way Violet had. He couldn't give the sheriff any reason to detain or arrest him, but the mama bear at his side had told the man where he could stick his thinly veiled threats, and Wyatt loved it.

The sheriff opened a notebook and took the bare minimum of information for his report, then left without a goodbye. He'd hooked mirrored sunglasses over his eyes, but there was no mistaking the downward twist to his lips. They'd really put him out by asking him to do his job.

Wyatt hated that guy.

He walked Violet inside and poured two fresh glasses of sweet tea. The others had grown warm and watered down with melted ice.

"What now?" Violet asked, drumming her thumbs against the kitchen table. "The sheriff obviously has no intention of helping us."

Wyatt rubbed his forehead. "I would have to agree with that assessment." He blew out a long breath and tried to refocus on something he could control. His investigation. "You said your grandma doesn't have a computer? Are you sure it wasn't stolen?" He retrieved his phone and checked the available Wi-Fi options. "I'm not picking up any networks." He moved through the rooms then, searching for signs of an internet cable.

Violet went to the old rolltop desk in the hallway and opened the filing drawer. "Grandma never had the internet while I lived here. I had a laptop for school, but I had to take it to the library or a café to get Wi-Fi." She sifted through the desk's contents for several minutes. "Nope." She waved a pair of white papers in the air. "These are Grandma's most recent phone and cable bills. Neither shows a charge for internet."

"Okay." Wyatt nodded. "I guess I can stop looking for a modem or router." He dialed the number for the body shop he'd passed in town, 555-BODY, and waited while it rang. "Let me see what I can do about our vehicles." He hung up partially satisfied. "I made arrangements for a new window installation and requested quotes for repainting your car, though I wouldn't recommend spending the money until we get to the bottom of whatever is wrong with this town."

Violet returned the papers to her grandma's desk, then leaned against the wall at its side. She stroked Maggie's tiny curls, her brow deeply furrowed. "Maybe Ruth has the internet. Grandma could've contacted you from Ruth's house." She pursed her lips, apparently not liking that explanation. "That reminds me," she said. "I saw Ruth again at the hospital, and she said she'd noticed Grandma hadn't been herself lately. She said she'd assumed it was because a friend of Grandma's has dementia and it's gotten a lot worse."

"I'm sorry to hear about her friend," Wyatt said. "What's her name?"

"Mary Alice. She's one of Grandma's closest friends, but a bit of a recluse." She dropped her palm onto a stack of novels piled on the desk.

"Oh!" Her eyes widened and her lips swept into a breathtaking smile. "I just figured out where Grandma used the internet."

AN HOUR LATER, Wyatt angled his truck into the lot at the local body shop and left his key with an attendant. The prices for repainting Violet's ten-year-old hatchback made buying a new one seem much more appealing.

Maggie had enjoyed a shaker of Cheerios on the drive over, and seemed ready for an adventure. Luckily, they had time to kill while the window was replaced, and according to Violet, the library wasn't far. She met him in the lot outside the body shop's office door, Maggie in a sling on her hip and a stack of her grandma's borrowed novels in her hands. "Ready?"

"After you." Wyatt scooped a hand through the air, indicating that she should lead the way.

They moved together along the narrow sidewalk. Traffic had picked up, and Wyatt walked closest to the curb, watching vigilantly for signs of trouble. Properties on both sides of the road were sprinkled with people. Some weeding flower beds, others rocking on a porch swing. Kids raced through sprinklers; others rode bikes with no hands or shot basketballs at netless rims bolted over closed garage doors. The occasional pickup truck trundled past, windows down and radio up.

"It's strange," Violet said. "Everything seems so normal from this perspective. It's exactly the way I remember this place, except that there's something bad circling us, and no one else seems to have a clue."

"It makes sense that no one knows what's going on," Wyatt said. "The attacks are pointed, and you're always alone when they happen. Whoever's doing these things wants to scare you away, not alert the whole town." He stepped into the street when the library came into view, then motioned Violet across. He moved like a crossing guard, watching both directions for signs of a blue-and-white derby car with an unhinged driver to appear.

"I guess," she said, arriving on the sidewalk outside the library. "I hate that Sheriff Masterson practically accused us of causing whatever problems we have. When will people like him stop blaming the victims?"

"People like him?" Wyatt asked. "Never." He followed Violet up the steps to a massive late-nineteenth-century building. Blue-gray clapboard covered the sides and a bright red door guarded the entry. A sign on the lawn declared the structure had once been home to the town's founder, built in 1864. A matching plaque beside the front door identified the historic estate as current home of the River Gorge Library.

Violet slipped inside and stopped at a large wooden desk. She stacked her grandma's borrowed novels into a tidy pile before her and smiled brightly at the woman behind the counter. "Hello, Mrs. Foster."

The librarian inched closer, gathering the books into her arms and squinting at Violet. She posed a pair of frameless glasses on the bridge of her nose and gasped. "Mercy!" She dropped the little pile of books onto the desk and pressed both palms to her narrow chest. "Violet Ames. It has been far too long. How are you? Come around here where I can see you."

Mrs. Foster met Violet along the side of the desk and hugged her tight. She leaned closer to coo at Maggie's face, then straightened for a look at Wyatt. "You must be the man I keep hearing about. Got some of the local women in a frenzy."

Violet barked a laugh.

Wyatt felt his cheeks heat stupidly. He offered her his hand. "Wyatt Stone. It's nice to meet you, ma'am."

She looked him over, then lifted her eyebrows at Violet.

Violet blushed. "Mrs. Foster, I was wondering if Grandma came in here recently to use the public computers?"

"Oh, yes. She's been here regularly for several weeks. How's she doing now? I heard she took a terrible spill. It's a shame. We get old, but we don't feel old. We do things we probably shouldn't."

"Like what?" Wyatt asked.

Mrs. Foster shrugged. "She was on a ladder in the barn, wasn't she? I threw my back out hauling Christmas decorations down from the attic last fall. I was laid up for two months. It happens. Lucky for her Ruth was there to find her. Living alone at our age is a dangerous business."

Violet chewed her bottom lip. "Do you know what she was using the computer for?"

"No." Mrs. Foster shook her head. "Recipes, I suppose. That's what I use them for."

"May I use one?" Violet asked.

"Sure thing."

Wyatt joined the women, winding through the aisles over creaky hardwood floors. Adult patrons relaxed on worn, antique-looking couches and armchairs arranged in little clusters. Children filled the floor space near the far wall, crowded around a woman in a cardboard crown reading from a tattered paperback.

"Here we are," Mrs. Foster said with a soft clap of her hands.

A bank of bulbous almond-colored computer monitors lined a series of tables. A hodgepodge of seating options stood in front of them. Mrs. Foster offered a stool to Violet, then dragged a rocking chair closer for Wyatt. "Here they are. Take as long as you need."

Wyatt stepped around the spindle rocker, certain he'd leave it in splinters if he tried to sit on it. "Do you know which computer Mrs. Ames preferred to use?"

he asked. People were often creatures of habit, and he hoped that Violet's grandma was no different.

"Of course." Mrs. Foster smiled. "She liked this one. It has a nice view of the front window. A good choice if you ask me."

A good choice, Wyatt thought, *if you were watching your back and didn't want to be cornered or confronted in a public library*. He cringed. If only she had met her attacker at the library instead of alone in her barn.

"Very few folks use these anymore," Mrs. Foster went on. "Everyone's got those smartphones and tablets. My great-nephew has both and he's in first grade." She looked sullen after uttering the words. "What's wrong with reading books?"

"We think Grandma was researching something," Violet said. "I'm hoping to find out what that was, so I can surprise her by finishing the job."

Wyatt moved in close to the machine and brought up the search history. "Do you keep a log of the users? Dates and times of use? The machine number? Anything like that?" If so, he could use the information to pinpoint what she was reading about online. From the looks of things, no one had deleted this unit's memory in a very long time.

"Of course. I'll be right back." Mrs. Foster hurried away in the direction that they'd come.

Violet stepped in close to Wyatt's side. "I didn't mean to say Grandma was researching anything. It just came out."

Wyatt forced a smile. "It's fine. Mrs. Foster seems nice, and you covered well."

The librarian returned with a clipboard. "I'm afraid I have to drop this off to you and run. Story time is over and Clary is being overrun with children demanding an encore."

They waited until Mrs. Foster had gone, then scanned the list.

"Wow," Violet said. "She's practically the only one on the list, and it looks like she came every morning for almost three weeks."

Wyatt scrolled through the machine's history, reviewing the links and pages that were visited each morning when Mrs. Ames was signed in. It was an unexpected list. "Was your grandpa a veteran?"

"Yes. William Ames," Violet answered. "Why?"

"She was searching military websites, Veterans Affairs and national cemeteries with military interments." Wyatt felt the creeping feeling of spiders on his skin. The fine hair on his neck and arms raised in warning. Almost as if they were being watched. He gave the room a careful look, then turned back to the job at hand. "She was researching a man named Henry Davis. Does that name ring a bell? A relative maybe?"

"No." Violet played with Maggie's fingers and stroked her cheeks. "I've never heard that name before. Maybe he was someone she knew when she was young? A neighbor?"

"Not a neighbor. This guy was from Twin Forks." Wyatt considered that a minute. "Twin Forks isn't far from here. Maybe they dated?"

"I don't know." Violet puffed air into her bangs. "I wish she'd just wake up and tell us what is happening.

We can't even be sure those searches have anything to do with her fall."

"True," Wyatt agreed, glad to hear her considering all avenues. "But the searches for my security firm are sandwiched between these every day for a month." He checked his surroundings again, hating the creeping sensation on his skin. "I don't know what it means, but I'm ready to get out of here. This guy, Davis, went missing nearly fifty years ago. Now seems like a strange time to start looking for him."

Violet's mouth opened. She shut it without saying whatever had come to mind. Maybe she was thinking the same thing Wyatt was. They needed to go.

"Hey." He stalled on a new series of other searches; this time Mrs. Ames had been researching a woman. "She was also looking for Mary Alice Grigsby."

Violet moved into the space at his side, staring at the list of websites and searches. "What about Mary Alice? Grandma has known her all her life. What could there be to look up?"

"I don't know. There's nothing here. Just searches for her name, and this one has a year. 1968." He checked the area for eavesdroppers and lookie-loos again. "I'm deleting the browsing history on this computer in case anyone comes in here asking the same questions we did. Henry Davis might be a lead, or it could be nothing, but considering the past few days' events, I'd rather cover our tracks."

"Agreed." Violet moved to the children's area and selected a few board books for Maggie, then went to check out.

Mrs. Foster greeted them. "Did you find what you were looking for on the computer?"

Wyatt leaned forward to fabricate a nonspecific cover-up, but Violet spoke first.

"Yes." She nodded, overly emphatic and oddly perky. "It looks like she really did want a kitten. I knew she had to be lonely living here by herself. She's been researching tabbies and local humane society adoption drives. I think I'll pick up a kitten for her and surprise her when she wakes up."

Mrs. Foster beamed, scanned the board books, then returned them to Violet. "That's so delightful of you. I wish my grandkids were as thoughtful. There now. I've put these on your grandma's library card. See you in two weeks?"

"Absolutely." Violet handed the books to Wyatt, then hurried back outside with him on her heels.

"Smooth," Wyatt said, more than a little impressed by her ability to think on her feet.

"Thanks. Now we just need to find out who Henry Davis is and why Grandma has been researching him all month. No problem." She rolled her eyes to emphasize the sarcasm, and Maggie laughed.

Wyatt pressed his cell phone to one ear. "I'm already on it."

A SHORT WALK for ice cream and the reading of a few board books on a park bench later, Wyatt received news that his window was fixed. Violet waited with Maggie outside the body shop office while he paid and collected his keys. The unsettling sensation of being watched hit her, sending chills across her skin and making her impossibly more antsy.

"Ready?" Wyatt asked, crossing to the driver's-side door.

Violet jumped. She'd been scanning the streets in search of the reason for her chills and missed his reappearance from the office. "Yes."

They climbed inside, ready to return home and process what they'd learned from the trip to the library.

Wyatt checked his mirrors and eased onto the road, then cast a wayward glance in her direction. "Everything okay?"

She rubbed the gooseflesh from her arm. "Just paranoia, I think." She watched the road, examined drivers in passing cars and searched the shadows of darkened alleyways as they made their way through the small downtown.

Soon, the buildings fell away, and they were back on the county road leading away from town and the hospital, toward her grandmother's house. The view was magnificent. The country in full bloom. Mountains lined the horizon. Forests reached into the heavens. And there with them, below the cloudless blue sky, were chasing squirrels, soaring birds and the occasional deer standing just inside the tree line at the roadside.

Violet watched the meandering river that cut through the valley below as the road sloped constantly lower, plummeting down the mountain. Her heart gave a painful thud as the deadly curve where she'd been run off the road came into view. She'd been going the other way, climbing up the hill, but she knew the curve, and just being near it tightened her limbs and jaw.

Wyatt slowed the truck and veered toward the shoulder. "Was that guardrail always busted like that?"

Violet leaned forward, straining for a clearer view. "No. I don't think so."

Wyatt pulled the truck onto the road's gravelly edge, stopping parallel to the torn and twisted guardrail.

Violet's eyes widened as a little red pickup came into view below, a wake of broken trees and flattened grasses stretching up the hill behind it.

Wyatt hit his flashers. "I'll be right back."

Violet watched in horror as he dashed over the mountainside to the truck, nearly standing on its crushed nose at the base of the ravine, just feet from the winding stream.

He pulled his phone from his pocket and caught it between his shoulder and ear while he wrenched open the driver's-side door.

"Someone is still in there," Violet whispered, realizing there was no other reason for Wyatt to open that door. Fear and panic lightened her head and heated her cheeks. She rolled down her window. "Can I help? What can I do?" she called.

Wyatt shook his head and raised a flat palm in her direction, indicating she should stay put. The low tenor of his voice carried in a mumble to her ears. He gave their location. The truck's description. Then the details of the driver. White female. Sixties or seventies. Deceased.

Violet opened her door. She gathered Maggie into

her arms and inched along the road's edge, suddenly terrified of being alone. Memories of the angry, roaring derby car slicked her palms and beaded sweat along her neck and forehead.

She took a few steady steps past the broken guardrail, keeping to the more level spaces between trees. Before she'd intended, she found herself at Wyatt's side, peering at the familiar female driver of the little red truck. Sickness coiled in Violet's core as the unseeing green eyes of her grandmother's friend Ruth stared back.

Chapter Seven

Wyatt rocked slowly on the front porch swing, fighting the memories of finding a nice old lady dead just hours earlier, and waiting for a return call from Sawyer at Fortress Security. If folks who knew Mrs. Ames were going to start turning up dead, Wyatt needed to get to the bottom of this mess fast, and Sawyer was the best man he knew at digging up buried information. Sawyer hadn't been a civilian as long as Wyatt, and he was having a tougher time adjusting, probably one more reason research jobs were his specialty. He got lost in them and frequently came out knowing more about his subjects than the people themselves. Sawyer was also excellent at reconnaissance. He was a ghost, and that was exactly what Wyatt needed. With Sawyer on the job, Wyatt could keep his focus on Violet and Maggie.

He stretched his long legs, pushing the silent swing back, then letting it glide forward once more. Shadows played on the horizon. Crickets and bullfrogs chirped and croaked in the distance. Lightning bugs rose from the grass. He listened closely to the night, picking up immediately on the sound of Violet's soft footfalls inside. The muted thuds of her return trip down the steps after putting Maggie into bed. Her daughter's jabbering voice carried softly through the baby monitor, presumably in Violet's hand.

"Hey." She opened the front door, toting the little white monitor.

Wyatt dropped a palm on the swing beside him. "Need a break?"

She accepted easily, setting the device on the armrest at her side. "Maggie's taking all this in stride," she said. "I could use a lesson."

"It helps when you have a strong mom to shelter you from the storm." Wyatt moved his arm across the swing's back, letting his hand dangle over Violet's shoulder. He fought the urge to drop it around her. Keeping up the pretense of their fabricated relationship in public was one thing. Touching her whenever the urge struck was downright unprofessional.

Violet stared into the night. "I can't believe Ruth is gone."

Wyatt considered offering a few words of comfort, but came up empty. What had happened to her grandma's friend was awful and the timing was incredibly worrisome.

"I think she was probably on her way from visiting Grandma," Violet said, "and I can't help wondering if that's why she had the accident. What if she was purposely run off the road?"

"The sheriff is looking into it," Wyatt said. "We'll know more soon."

Violet turned fearful blue eyes up to him. "That could have been Maggie and me."

The monitor at Violet's side glowed brighter. A series of tiny arching lights circled the speaker, illuminating with Maggie's every babble, responding to the decibel and urgency of her calls. At the moment it was slow and tired baby talk.

Despite the tense mood, a smile pulled at Wyatt's mouth. He couldn't help it. He'd love to know what that little nugget was yammering about. "She's got to be beat," Wyatt said. "It was a hot one, and she spent plenty of time in the sun."

Violet gathered her hair into a loose ponytail and sighed. "Nearly ten thirty at night, and it's still a hot one." She released her dark brown locks, and they fell over her shoulders once more, releasing an intoxicating vanilla scent before landing briefly on his hand, then sliding away. "Any word from your partner?"

"No. Not yet." He dared a look into her tired, defeated eyes. "We will figure this out." He tapped her shoulder with his dangling hand. "That's a promise."

Violet pursed her lips. "Okay." She pulled her feet onto the swing and tucked them beneath her, erasing the bit of distance that had existed between their bodies. Her head fell against his shoulder.

Wyatt's heart expanded at the gesture and her answer. *Okay.* Those two syllables suddenly meant everything. There was no doubt in her tone. No question. Just *okay*. She trusted him to fulfill his promise, and he would. His heart gave a powerful tug, and a fresh realization knocked him over the head like an anvil. That juiced-up protective instinct, the urge to touch her, comfort her, see her smile…the desire to make Maggie laugh, to be near her, to be with them both… Wyatt had begun to think of these ladies as if they were *his* to protect. Not just as if it was his job to keep them safe, but as if he was protecting what was already his.

"I put on some coffee," she said. "I doubt I'll be able to sleep. Not after a lunatic marched right onto the property to carve up my car. So I thought I could stay downstairs with you, keep watch."

Spend the night with him? That was her offer? Wyatt struggled to organize his thoughts. "You should sleep. You're exhausted, and Maggie needs you to bring your mommy A game." He forced a smile. He doubted Violet would accept the advice for her own good, but he had a feeling she'd do anything so long as it was for Maggie. "I'll keep watch."

"What do you think will happen if I don't *go home*?" She deepened her voice on the final two words, a mockery of the vandal's voice, Wyatt assumed with a grin.

"You can, you know," he said. "I can handle things here if you think you'd be safer at home." He hated the words, but they were true and already out of his traitorous mouth.

"I've thought of leaving," she said. "I've tried to guess what would be best for Maggie, but I can't. Something awful is happening here, but what if whoever is behind all these terrible things thinks I know something I shouldn't? What if he thinks I've uncovered what Grandma knew? Or that she'd told me what she was up to before her fall? How can I be sure her assailant will just let me go home and forget about it? What if his goal is to separate me from you? Will I be in more danger without your protection?" Her blue eyes pleaded with Wyatt for answers. "I don't want to be the naive little woman who runs headlong into trouble only to discover she was safer here all along."

Wyatt's heart broke for her. He hated the fear in her eyes and the questions he couldn't answer. He hated that criminals and evil existed in the world. It was the very reason he and Sawyer had founded Fortress Security.

The lights on the monitor flickered, glowing brightly as Maggie squealed. The sound was momentarily audible through the home's open front door as well as the little speaker. The lights dimmed, and she gave out a long weary groan.

Violet straightened slightly, shifting away from Wyatt. "She's okay. I call this portion of the bedtime routine 'singing herself to sleep.'"

Wyatt listened more closely to the strange moaning sound. Not crying, but not babbling. Just a low stretching lament. "You might consider voice lessons," he suggested.

Violet elbowed his ribs playfully. "First she's too negative for you, and now she can't sing? I think your expectations are too high, Wyatt Stone."

"I've heard that before," he admitted. His gaze returned to the little monitor. How had a man left this woman and his sweet baby? A military man. A man who was supposed to live by a code of honor. It wasn't right, and yet if that's who the guy was, maybe it was best he wasn't around to influence that little girl. She deserved better. They both did.

"What?" Violet shifted at his side, frowning.

"Nothing." Violet's ex was none of his business. Wyatt pulled his gaze away from the monitor, fixed it on her sincere blue eyes instead.

"Something," she pushed. "What were you thinking? Be straight with me. I need to know what's going on here. All of it. Not the filtered version, either. If you know something you haven't told me…" She trailed off. "Please."

"I'm sorry Maggie's daddy left," he blurted. "That's all I was thinking, and I know it's none of my business."

Her brows rose.

Wyatt groaned inwardly and braced for her rebuff. He wasn't great with words or timing. Being a straight shooter was perfect for military life, but it was a continuous train wreck as a civilian. "I'm sorry. You asked."

Violet shifted again, putting as much space as possible between them on the small swing. An inch. Maybe two; given the swing's size and his, it was a miracle to find as much space as she did. "Thanks, but we're fine."

"I can see that. I still hate that he left." Wyatt rubbed his palms down the thighs of his jeans. "It's not right, and I can't understand it."

She studied him. "I was reckless with my heart. That's on me."

Wyatt bit his tongue, forcing his mouth to be still before it got him into trouble. What had happened to

Violet wasn't her fault, but he doubted he could convince her otherwise. Violet was strong. Determined. Maggie was lucky. And Violet's ex was a full-fledged idiot.

Violet deflated, rolling her back against the swing. She ran the pads of her thumbs beneath her eyes.

Was she crying? His gut fisted. Had he done that? "Hey." Wyatt planted his feet against the porch boards, stopping the swing. "I didn't mean to be rude. I just think you both deserve better."

"It's not you," she said. "The last two days are catching up with me. That's all." She heaved a sigh, then dropped her hands onto her lap. "I want to see Grandma again tomorrow. I wish I'd asked Ruth about Henry Davis. Maybe Grandma told her something useful." Maybe that was the reason Ruth's family was now planning a funeral.

Wyatt offered a remorseful smile. "I'll drive this time."

"All right."

"About what you said earlier," Wyatt began, "we don't know if you and Maggie will be safer by staying or going, but if you stay I can promise not to leave your side."

"If we stay, will it keep you from your investigation? Finding out who did this to Grandma should be your first priority. Not us. We're extra. Not what you negotiated in the contract."

He lifted his cell phone from the armrest beside him. "This is all I need. If there's a cell tower, I can work. And Violet?"

"Yeah?"

"I don't give a damn about that contract."

She smiled. "Okay."

His phone buzzed against his palm with an incoming text. "See?" he said, smiling as he lifted his phone. "Work." He swiped the screen to life and read the message from Sawyer.

"What?" Violet sat taller, apparently seeing the shock on his face.

"When I spoke with Sawyer earlier, he wondered if your grandma had been researching on behalf of her friend with dementia. Sawyer's grandpa had Alzheimer's, and he said those patients often recall things far in the past as clearly as, or more clearly than, things that happened yesterday. He thought maybe Mary Alice had asked your grandma about something, and your grandma went to look it up."

Violet puckered her brow. "That's possible." She motioned to the phone in Wyatt's hand. "But why do you look like the phone is burning you?"

Wyatt reworked his expression. "I asked Sawyer to look into Mary Alice Grigsby, and he learned that she was married later the same year Henry Davis went missing."

"So?"

"Her married name is Mary Alice Masterson."

AIR WHOOSHED FROM Violet's lungs. She'd known Mary Alice's last name, but Wyatt hadn't. "Of course." Why hadn't she made the connection before? "Mary Alice is the sheriff's mom." And Grandma's friend. "Is it possible Mary Alice told Grandma something meant to be a secret?"

"Maybe," Wyatt said.

Violet's thoughts whirled. Was Mary Alice's relationship to the sheriff relevant to the derby car or Grandma's accident? To Ruth's death?

Wyatt's phone buzzed again. "Email," he said, motioning her to move in closer. He flicked his thumb over the screen and opened the new message.

Breath caught in her throat at the subject line. *Henry Davis.*

Wyatt clicked the link in the message, rerouting them to an article from the neighboring county's newspaper dated 1968. A twenty-three-year-old soldier, Henry Davis, was presumed AWOL when he didn't return for duty after a brief leave. His last known whereabouts was a concert in Grove County.

"River Gorge is in Grove County," Violet whispered. She set her head back against the top wooden slat of the swing when she finished reading. Her heart kicked and spluttered in her chest as facts from the seemingly irrelevant article played in her mind. Nothing made any sense. Not even the gentle giant seated beside her, more worried about her comfort and safety than the mystery at hand. She'd overheard him earlier, telling his partner that he couldn't manage the research this time. He'd said Violet and Maggie were his priorities, and he hadn't called Maggie "the baby" or "Violet's daughter," the way most people did. He'd called her Maggie and Violet loved the way it had sounded. Wyatt, a virtual mammoth compared to her tiny daughter, saw Maggie as a person. Not an accessory to Violet. Not a possession to be protected or managed. A person. Violet saw that same truth manifested in Wyatt's actions. He worried when she fussed, and he made silly faces to calm her when she was mad. He was kind and loving.

Violet gripped the knotted muscles over one shoulder and squeezed. She couldn't afford to care about Wyatt's kindness. She couldn't take it personally. He was a nice man who was doing his job. Violet was a single mom who needed to get her head straight about what was real and what was fantasy. Having a family for Maggie, like the one Violet had never had—that was fantasy.

She excused herself, opting to stew over her naivety alone. Forget the coffee. She needed to rest and reboot her tired mind.

Hours later, sunlight drifted through the parted curtains, waking Violet with a start. Dust motes danced and floated on the air above her head, suspended like iridescent confetti. A smile touched her lips. Her gaze darted to the alarm clock on the nightstand. It was after eight. Maggie must've been as tired as her mama. She never slept past six. The baby monitor was dark. Powered off. Violet rolled onto her side for a look into the pop-up playpen.

Maggie was gone.

Violet was on her feet. "Wyatt!" She bulleted down the steps toward the kitchen. Slowed quickly by the familiar sounds of nursery rhymes and Maggie shouting, "No!" As the kitchen came into view, so did her daughter, head thrown back in laughter.

Wyatt waved a spatula at her from his place at the stove. "Eggs and toast again. I'm a one-hit wonder."

Violet padded over the cool linoleum floor to stand beside Maggie's high chair. She kissed her head and caught her breath. "The monitor was off. She was gone." Her fingers curled against the table. For a moment, she'd thought the worst. Forgotten there was someone else in the house. Someone good.

"She was babbling and chattering on about nothing for a long while," he said. "When you didn't jump right up like yesterday, I assumed you needed the sleep." A mass of deep lines ran over his forehead. "Was that wrong?" Wyatt's dark gaze shifted from Violet to Maggie, then back once more. "I didn't mean to scare you." Color ran from his face and a look of discontentment settled where congeniality had been moments before. "I thought you'd hear us as soon as you woke. Hear her laughter. Start your day with some extra sleep and a smile."

Violet rubbed her eyes. "No. It's fine. I guess." Was it? She had no idea. No one had ever helped her before, and Wyatt was practically a stranger. Right? Maybe she'd been right to push the bed against the door on that first night.

She shuffled to the coffeepot and poured a large mug of steaming clarity. Though she wasn't sure how much it would take to make this visit to River Gorge any less confusing than it already was. "Did you learn anything new about Henry Davis?" She rested her backside against the countertop and sucked hot coffee into her system.

"Not yet. I asked Sawyer to check his military records. It looks like he never went back after his leave. Could have gone AWOL intentionally. Lots of folks didn't believe in the war then. He could've assumed a new identity and vanished. Whatever happened was permanent. Sawyer said Henry's parents eventually had him declared legally dead, so they could have a memorial service. Sawyer's going to try to contact his next of kin and see if anyone has heard family gossip about what might've happened to him. His folks are long dead now, but there could be children, nieces, nephews, siblings."

The landline rang, and Violet jumped. She rubbed the goose bumps off her arms. "Maybe that's the hospital," she said, hurrying to the wall to answer. "Hello?"

"Um, yes," a shaky female voice began. "Violet?"

"Yes. This is Violet."

"Oh, good. Well, this is Mrs. Foster." She paused. "From the library. I have those other books you requested."

"I didn't request—"

"Yes, that's right," Mrs. Foster cut her off. "They're here now, so you should come on down and pick them up."

Violet's gaze swept the room, landing on Wyatt's blank face. "Now?"

"Yes. Now would be fine, dear."

Violet felt fear pool in her stomach and fix her feet in place. She'd been awake for ten minutes and already something else was wrong. "I'll be there as soon as I can."

"Darling?" Mrs. Foster added hastily, a bit louder this time. "Bring your friend."

The line went dead and Violet whirled on Wyatt. "That was Mrs. Foster. We need to go to the library. Now."

Chapter Eight

Violet hurried up the steps to the library. It was barely 9:00 a.m., and the library wasn't slated to open until ten, but the lights were all on inside. She cradled Maggie in her sling as she jogged, heart and mind sprinting with concerns for what awaited her beyond the historic red door.

Mrs. Foster met them at the threshold, swinging the door wide and motioning Violet and Wyatt inside. "Thank you for coming." She pressed the door shut behind them and slid the lock into place. "I'm sorry I behaved so strangely on the phone, but I was worried, and I didn't know what else to do. Now that I've had a moment to relax, I wonder if I've wasted your time."

"What worried you?" Wyatt asked. "And for the record, you can call anytime."

"Yes," Violet agreed. "It's no trouble for us to be here. What happened?"

Mrs. Foster wet her thin white lips. "Sheriff Masterson was here this morning when I arrived at eight. I came early to tidy up and restock shelves. It's too hard to get to it once we open. I won't have any help here until afternoon." She splayed thin fingers over her collarbone, a tremor playing on her narrow frame.

Violet inched closer. "You don't look well," she said, sliding a steady hand down the librarian's arm, shoulder to elbow. "Can I get you some water? Would you like to sit down?"

Mrs. Foster nodded, then moved to the nearest table and took a seat. "I'll be fine. Like I said, I've surely overreacted. After what's happened to your grandma, and now Ruth, I can't help feeling as if I'm living in an episode of *The Twilight Zone*."

Violet took the seat across from Mrs. Foster, then set Maggie on the floor, keeping an eye on her as she crawled to the nearest chair and tried to pull herself up. She'd dressed her little princess in a red-and-white-checkered sundress, complete with lace-rimmed socks and ruffles across the little white bloomers beneath. All she needed was a pair of cowgirl boots to complete the outfit, but Violet had forgotten them, rushing through her routine to get to the library. It was okay, she assured herself. The pediatrician had said babies learning to stand and walk do better in bare feet than in soled shoes. Of course, Maggie wasn't walking yet, but she tried getting onto her feet at every opportunity.

Wyatt crept along with Maggie staying a step behind as she moved chair to chair, grabbing hold and failing to get completely upright before moving on. "Why was Sheriff Masterson here?" he asked Mrs. Foster. "You say he was waiting for you when you arrived?"

"Yes," she said, then frowned. "Well, no. I didn't mean the current Sheriff Masterson. I meant the former one. Tom Sr. That man was sheriff so long I think I've gotten the title in my head like it's part of his name."

Violet glanced at Wyatt. "Mary Alice's husband was the sheriff before her son, but I've never met the man."

"Well, you haven't missed out on anything," Mrs. Foster said. "If you've met Tom Jr., then you'd know apples don't fall far from their trees." She folded her hands on one knee, crinkling the material of her simple brown-and-white print dress. "They're both about as friendly as an alley cat, but Tom Sr. is harder. He's always made me nervous, and he seems to have taken up drinking, which made it worse this morning. I imagine life's been tough on him since Mary Alice was diagnosed with dementia, but it's barely 9:00 a.m." She fiddled with her skirt, looking suddenly sad. "It was rough on everyone when Mary Alice's slow decline took a plummet last month. We all knew it was coming, of course. That's the nature of the disease, but how do you prepare for something like that?" She shook her head sadly.

Violet's heart broke for Mary Alice and all the folks who loved her. "What did Mr. Masterson want today?"

"He wanted to come inside and take a look at the computers, so I let him. I'm not even sure if I could have said no. He was the sheriff for years. Decades. When I smelled the gin on his breath, I got worried. Then I thought about how odd it was for him to come this morning asking about the same thing you did yesterday. Especially since your grandma and his wife are so close, and one is ill and the other is in the hospital. Maybe I read too much Agatha Christie. I don't know, but the timing, and the way he showed up here for the first time ever, as far as I know, and two hours before we open, set off my internal alarm bells." She scrunched her face. "That's silly, right?"

"No," Wyatt said. "It's perceptive and smart."

Violet scooted to the edge of her seat. "He asked about the same thing we did? Do you mean my grandma?"

"Yes." She wrung her hands.

"Did he say what he was looking for, specifically?" Wyatt asked.

"No. He just wanted to know if Mrs. Ames had used the computers and if anyone else had come in asking about her. I said no to both." Her cheeks darkened in humility. "I don't normally lie."

Violet offered a small smile. "It's okay. You were scared and alone with a man who'd clearly been drinking. Anyone would have acted out of character in that situation."

Mrs. Foster lowered her eyes. "Thank you for saying that."

"It's true," Violet assured. "What else can you tell us?"

"Not much. I asked him how Mary Alice was doing. He said fine. When he asked if your grandma had been in to use the computers, I told him she'd fallen and was in the hospital. He didn't respond to that. He just marched on past me and flopped onto a chair at one of the computers. That was when I called you."

Wyatt took another small side step, following Maggie around the table. "Did you know Mary Alice and Tom before they were married?"

"Loosely," she said. "I met Mary Alice at a bonfire in Potter's Field. It was a big hangout in those days. We stayed friends for a little while after that. As long as we could, I mean."

"Any reason it didn't last?" Wyatt asked.

Mrs. Foster let her gaze fall briefly to the floor, clearly uncomfortable rehashing other folks' personal stories, yet still visibly unnerved by her morning run-in with the former sheriff. She pulled her attention determinedly back to Wyatt. "Once she was married, things changed. She'd longed to be out of her parents' home so she would be free to do what she wanted, but moving in with her new husband was worse. When they returned from their honeymoon, he practically isolated her. Once they had children, she barely left home. Most of her friends moved on. We still chatted when she came in for new books each week. I enjoyed that time very much, but it was always limited. He was always outside waiting in the car. Your grandmother hung on, though. She refused to let Mary Alice slip away into isolation. After the dementia diagnosis, your grandmother was practically the only person Tom would let in the door."

Wyatt crossed his arms. "Sounds like the Mastersons have been in power a long time. Let's hope neither man is behind all the lawbreaking."

Maggie made it to Violet's chair and grabbed her mom's calves, trying and failing to pull herself upright. Violet lifted her onto her lap for a kiss.

Wyatt relaxed his stance and turned his full attention on Mrs. Foster. "May I take a look at the computers again? I'm not sure what there is to find, but I'm curious about what Mr. Masterson looked up while he was here."

"Help yourself," she said with a flip of one wrist. "I'm just glad he's gone. His son came to pick him up a few minutes before you got here. I'm not sure how he knew where to find him, but he removed him through the back door service exit. I suppose it would've been embarrassing to be caught hauling your drunken father away from the library at eight thirty in the morning."

Maggie wiggled, and Violet set her back onto the floor. She flipped immediately into a crawl and headed off in the direction Wyatt had gone.

"Mrs. Foster?" Violet asked, a new question popping into mind. "Does the name Henry Davis mean anything to you?"

Mrs. Foster paused. She frowned. "It sounds vaguely familiar. I'm not sure why."

"He's a military man from Grove County who went missing in 1968. He was twenty-three at the time."

"Oh my. That would make him my age now." She cupped one palm over her jawline. "No. I can't place the name. I'm the wrong person to ask. I didn't get out of River Gorge often as a young woman. Is he still missing?"

"I'm not sure."

Wyatt's head appeared to bob over the aisles of books as he strode back into view. Brown eyes deep in thought. He'd dressed in low-slung jeans and a fitted gray T-shirt that accentuated his body in knee-buckling ways. The set to his jaw made Violet want to run her finger along it, maybe also her lips. "There were no recent searches on any of the computers," he said. "Makes me wonder if he might've come in just to check the search history like we did."

Mrs. Foster looked ill. She let her hands fall onto the table. "I didn't watch. I wanted to put some distance between us, so I went to the desk and called you. It just didn't feel right, him being here like that."

Violet leaned across the table and squeezed Mrs. Foster's fingers. She understood the unsettling feeling, the uncertainty and fear, not knowing if there was real danger or if she couldn't trust her instincts anymore.

"What do you think he wanted?" the librarian asked. "What's all this about? First you, then Tom. It isn't about buying your grandma a cat."

"No." Violet offered a sad smile, though she was unwilling to tell Mrs. Foster any more than she absolutely had to. There was no reason to drag her into Grandma's mess any further than they already had. She lifted her gaze to Wyatt's grim expression. Was it too late?

"Where's Maggie?" Wyatt asked. He twisted at the waist, examining the immediate area. "Can you see her?"

"No." Violet slid her chair away from the table, nearly toppling it in her haste. Her heart lodged instantly, painfully, in her throat. "She went after you."

Wyatt spun on his boots and launched into a sprint, heading back in the direction he'd come. "I don't see her," he called. "She's not here."

"Maggie!" His voice boomed over the rows of book-laden shelves.

"Oh dear." Mrs. Foster went toward the front door. "I'll check behind the reference desk."

Violet forced her leaden feet into action. She ran the length of the long room at half speed, ducking to peep under tables and slowing to peer down each empty aisle. "Maggie?"

Wyatt fell into step at her side a moment later. "She's not in the back. Not near the computers, in the bathrooms or activity space."

"Maggie!" Violet hollered, more loudly, more desperately. She raked shaky fingers through her hair, gripping her skull and trying to think. "She's a baby. She can't have walked away."

"Right," Wyatt agreed. "She's not tall enough to reach doorknobs, and there are no more open doors. The library isn't open yet, so there are no patrons to take her, and there's nothing to get hurt on." Wyatt ticked off perfectly good reasons for Violet to remain calm. "So let's split up and start again."

"She's not here," Violet said, rubbing the heavy ache in her chest. "We've already looked. Something's happened to her. She's in trouble. I feel it. I know it! Maggie!" She turned in a slow contemplative circle. The back door stood silently before her. "Mrs. Foster said the sheriff took his dad out this way."

"She can't open that," Wyatt said. "Even if it's unlocked."

"Yeah?" Violet sprinted for the door. "And what if

someone took her?" She thrust her weight against the heavy door, and it burst open. Unlocked.

No, Maggie definitely couldn't have opened the door, Violet thought as she squinted against the sun in search of the sheriff or maybe the blue-and-white derby car, but an adult could have.

A red-and-white-checked sundress scuttled swiftly through the distant grass.

"No!" Violet flew from the door, hitting the parched earth at a run. "Maggie! No!"

Her baby was closing the distance to the sidewalk and headed for a very busy street.

Chapter Nine

"Maggie!" Violet raced for the road, adrenaline forcing her forward faster than her legs could keep up. Her feet tangled and she fell, jamming her palms against hard, unforgiving earth. "Stop!" Tears streamed from her eyes as she regained herself. The plea was little more than a choked cry and she pushed her shaken frame upright. "Stop!"

Maggie slowed to look over her shoulder. The skirt of her little red-and-white dress fluttered in the breeze.

Violet was back in motion. "Baby, wait! Wait for Mommy!"

Maggie smiled. She turned back for the road, drawn to a plastic bag caught on a manhole cover and billowing like a balloon. The bag vanished and reappeared, repeatedly crushed by passing cars, only to reinflate with the next warm dose of wind.

"Maggie!" Wyatt's voice blasted through the air. He flew past Violet in long steady strides. "Whoa now." He skidded to a stop between Maggie and the road.

Violet froze in place. Her frantic mind nearly collapsed in relief.

Wyatt swept her baby into his arms and carried her back to Violet, easily delivering the beautiful child to her mother.

"Thank you." Violet sobbed against her baby, cuddling her, snuggling her. "I'm so sorry," she cried. "I shouldn't have taken my eyes off of you. I love you so much. I'm so very sorry."

Maggie whimpered and squirmed, then let out a heartbreaking wail.

"Oh my goodness." Violet wiped frantically at her face. "Now I've scared her." She groaned. "Shhh. It's okay." She bounced Maggie in her arms and fought the powerful wave of emotion pushing against her barely held composure.

A strong arm curved around her back, offering strength where she had none. Wyatt nudged her toward the library. "This wasn't your fault," he said. His voice was thick with promise and resolute determination. "You had no reason to worry. You couldn't have known." He moved slowly, steadfastly, at her side, matching his pace to her much slower one. "Let's take a minute. Get some water. Then I think it's time we pay Mary Alice and Tom Masterson Sr. a visit."

Violet swallowed hard. Her tongue felt swollen and sticky. She could definitely use a glass of water, but she wasn't sure she was ready to see Tom Masterson. If he had anything to do with what had happened to Maggie, he might be the next one in the hospital.

Wyatt helped her back into the library. He explained what had happened and warned Mrs. Foster to be careful. He got directions to the Masterson home while Violet calmed Maggie and herself with interchanged lullabies and Lamaze breathing. Her heart swelled with thanks and appreciation for him by the second. Not just for saving her daughter, but for being strong when she couldn't. For keeping a level head and for trudging forward to learn the truth and stop this criminal when Violet only wanted to run and hide.

She fastened Maggie into the five-point safety harness of her rear-facing car seat, then checked the belt a dozen times for security before joining Wyatt on the pickup's front bench. "I can't believe that just happened," she croaked, still strangled by residual fear. "Who would do something like that? To run me off the road or scratch up my car is one thing. That's a hands-off crime. A jerk move. But to creep into a building with three adults and steal a baby." She smashed her mouth shut, unable to voice the rest aloud.

To carry an infant away from her mother and leave her alone and unprotected, where anyone could hurt or abduct her. Where any manner of horrific fate awaited her.

The image of her baby nearing the busy downtown street flooded fresh into her mind. A hot tear rolled over her cheek. "It's pure evil."

Wyatt slid a large calloused hand across the seat between them and gripped Violet's fingers. He didn't speak. He just held tight, pulling cautiously into traffic, his trusty Stetson tipped low on his forehead.

Violet curled her fingers in response, gently squeezing him back.

WYATT SLID HIS truck against the curb outside a well-maintained craftsman-style home on Ridge Road. Mrs. Foster wasn't able to recall the exact address, but she'd described the place to a T, right down to the American flag waving proudly over the broad front porch. "Ready?" he asked Violet, in no hurry to release her small hand.

"Not at all," she said, slowly unfurling her fingers from his. "I have no proof that the man who lives here took my baby and left her outside the library, but I still want to slug him. Hard. And a lot."

Wyatt fought a smile. "Me, too. But you're right. We have no idea what really happened, so we can't make assumptions, and we need to go at this gently. Search for answers, not revenge. Not yet," he added. Though he certainly wouldn't be opposed to a little painful restitution for whomever had taken Maggie.

Violet turned heated eyes on him, frowning deeply. "Fine. But if he's behind this, I'm hitting him. I don't care if we find out today or on Maggie's sixtieth birthday."

Wyatt extended a fist her way to lighten the mood. "I accept those terms."

She bumped her tiny hand against his, then lifted wiggling fingers in the air.

Wyatt laughed. "Okay. Get out. That was too corny to happen in my truck." His smile grew as he watched her. The strange and unfamiliar tug returned to his chest and gut. He admired her, he realized. He was proud of the way she stood up for herself and fought for her daughter, and for the way she kept moving forward when others would've fallen down.

Violet opened her door with a straight face. "I was the Queen of Corn once, you know?"

He joined her outside the vehicle as she loaded Maggie into her sling. "Still are, I think."

Maggie drooped against Violet's side, having exhausted herself crying.

"No. I was the actual Queen of Corn. I rode on a float in the Harvest Day Parade and everything."

"Good grief." Wyatt feigned horror. "You can't keep things like that bottled up. They'll fester."

The screen door of the home creaked open on heavy springs, then snapped shut, drawing their attention to the porch ahead of them. A frail-looking woman in a housecoat and curlers shuffled out. She carried a bag of yarn to the nearest rocker and lowered herself slowly into it, resting the bag at her feet. She positioned a set of giant needles on her lap, then tugged a fuzzy blue strand of yarn from the bag until it lay limply over her legs.

Wyatt dipped his head to Violet's ear. "Is that Mary Alice?"

"Yes." Violet paused, watching the woman. "She used to be so plump and vibrant," she whispered.

The woman began to rock and knit. She hummed tunelessly as she worked, oblivious to the pair standing on her sidewalk.

Violet slid her arm beneath Wyatt's and curved her hand around his biceps. She led him to the woman's front porch steps, but stopped short of climbing them. "Mary Alice?"

The woman's hands froze, stilling her busy needles. She lifted her head first, then moved milky blue eyes in search of Violet.

Wyatt shrugged off the willies. Obviously, the woman was ill, but the look on her face was distant and haunting. Besides that, he couldn't see into her home despite an open door. The rooms were cloaked in shadow thanks to a bright morning sun. It would have eased Wyatt's nerves to know where drunk Tom Sr. was at the moment. Passed out, hopefully. Wyatt didn't like the idea of walking into potentially hostile territory without a better plan than ask questions and see what happens. Still, how could they plan for this? A conversation with a woman suffering the way Mary Alice was?

"Hello," the woman said. She seemed to reanimate after a long moment of studying Violet. "It's a beautiful day."

"Yes, it is," Violet said. "How are you feeling?"

"Oh, very well, thank you. I'm knitting a blanket for Tom. It gets cold at night, you know?"

Violet slid her eyes toward Wyatt.

He could practically hear her thoughts. It had been a low of eighty-three degrees last night. He'd slept in as little as possible with every window open. Mary Alice was confused. Not exactly a great interviewee, but he nudged Violet to keep going. Confused or not, Mary Alice was all they had to go on at the moment.

She turned a bright smile on the older woman. "I hope we aren't disturbing you. Is Tom home now?"

Another sign Violet could read minds. Wyatt looked to Mary Alice, needing the answer to that question.

She went back to work on her blanket. "No. He's at work. He takes afternoon shifts so he can be with me and the baby all day."

Wyatt rubbed a palm across his forehead, collecting beads of sweat along the way. There were so many things wrong with her statement. She thought she had a baby? That her husband was at work, not retired? And apparently she also wasn't clear about the time. Barely 10:00 a.m. Not afternoon or evening.

Mary Alice lifted her gaze suddenly and affixed it to Violet. "Is that your new granddaughter, Gladys?" she asked. "Shame your daughter ran off on her like that. Better for Violet, probably, but tough on you." She shook her head, looking forlorn.

Violet loosened her grip on Wyatt's arm.

Mary Alice thought Violet was her grandmother? And Maggie was Violet?

Wyatt covered her hand with his, keeping it there. He gave her fingers an extra squeeze for reassurance. He felt guilty for being exposed to secrets he hadn't asked for, but Violet should know he'd never pass judgment. He didn't care who had raised her or why. He was there for her and Maggie.

Violet lifted a palm to shade the sun from her eyes. "I'm Violet," she said. "This is my daughter, Maggie, and my boyfriend, Wyatt."

Wyatt's shoulder's squared at her proclamation.

Mary Alice went back to humming.

He dropped his hand away then, stunned by the realization that he'd become impossibly, unprofessionally attached to Violet and her baby.

Violet released him in turn, wrapping her arms around her sleeping baby instead. "Mary Alice, do you remember Henry Davis?" she asked flatly, obviously ruffled by Mary Alice's mention of her mother.

Mary Alice raised a death glare in response. "I told you to never say that name. It was a secret. My secret. Not yours. You aren't supposed to talk about him."

"I'm sorry," Violet stuttered.

Wyatt tented his brows, unsure what to say to that or what her fevered words had meant.

"I didn't mean to say it," Violet went on. "I forgot. Please forgive me?"

Mary Alice jerked her chin woodenly up and down. Her knitting needles jammed and poked at the yarn, no longer working in peaceful harmony or with a skilled grip. "I told you not to say it. I told you never to tell anyone. Have you told him?" She flickered an angry gaze toward Wyatt.

"No," Violet promised. "I swear it. I only came by because I'm having trouble remembering things, and I thought you could help me."

Wyatt shifted his weight, leaning and peering around the home in each direction, listening for signs Mr. Masterson was on his way to break up the chitchat and kick them off his property.

Mary Alice's angry expression faltered. "Me, too," she said.

"It's hard." Violet sighed long and loud. "I hate it."

"Me, too."

"If only I could remember about Henry Davis," she said.

Mary Alice threw her yarn down at her feet. "I said stop it."

Violet started. She leaned closer to Wyatt, as if the old lady might become a threat.

He leaned into her, supporting her. "Go on," he whispered, "you've got this. Rewind a little and take it slow."

She straightened with a long exhale. "Sorry," she apologized again. "I keep forgetting. I don't mean to."

Mary Alice's eyes widened. She hunched forward, resting bony elbows against her thighs. "You haven't forgotten where you put it? Have you?"

"It?" Violet asked. "I think I have. Do you know where I put it?"

"No!" Mary screamed the word. She jerked upright and paced the porch, tugging at her clothes. "You said you'd keep it safe. You promised! And now you've lost it?"

"I don't know," Violet pleaded. "I can't remember what it is. I might know where I put it. What was it? Tell me," she urged.

Mary Alice stopped to look more closely at Violet. She examined Maggie, then Wyatt.

He wondered what she saw. Mary Alice was the first person he'd encountered in a long while who was a complete and unpredictable mystery to him. Sadly, probably also to herself.

She lifted the material of her housecoat, stared at her hands, the porch, the sky. Then she dropped her face into waiting palms and sobbed. "I don't know what's happening."

"Mary?" A deep tenor exploded into the air. "Mary?" The thunder of racing footsteps underscored the bellow. "I'm here. I'm coming." The screen door whipped open again, sending Mary Alice against the railing with a squeal.

A tall gray-haired man with broad shoulders and lean build pulled her into his arms. He rocked her clumsily. Probably still drunk from the morning gin, Wyatt assumed. "What's wrong, honey?" he rasped. His drooping lids shaded red-rimmed eyes.

"I don't know," she said. Her words were muffled against his chest. "I can't remember."

The man straightened, taking notice of Wyatt, Violet and Maggie. "Who are you? What are you doing on my property?" His red pocketed T-shirt was torn at the sleeve and slightly askew. His faded blue jeans hung low on his hips. The hems puddled around bare feet, too long without a belt and shoes. "Did you do this?" he barked. "Did you make her cry?" His meaty hands rolled into fists against Mary Alice's back.

His words were fired quickly, but sloppy from drink. He narrowed his eyes on Maggie. His mouth opened again, but he didn't speak.

Shocked, Wyatt thought. *He recognizes Maggie.*

Wyatt fought the urge to lash out, to force Violet and Maggie into his truck and come back to get answers from this man privately and by force. "Sir," he began calmly instead. "I'm Wyatt Stone. This is my girlfriend, Violet Ames, and her daughter, Maggie. We're in town because Violet's grandma was in an accident. She's at the hospital now. Been there a couple days."

Mary Alice wrenched in her husband's arms. "What?"

"My grandma fell," Violet said. "I don't know how she fell, but she's not waking up." The pain in her voice was a punch to Wyatt's chest.

Mary Alice's eyes seemed to clear. She lifted her chin, searching her husband's face. Mary Alice was back in the moment.

Tom Sr. registered the change in her, as well. He gripped her forearms firmly and lowered himself until their eyes were level. "What did they ask you? What did you say?"

"Nothing," she gasped, tugging uselessly against his hold. "I don't know."

"Why were you yelling? Crying?"

Mary Alice pulled free. Stunned, she lifted her fingers to her dampened cheeks. "I was crying?"

"Damn it!" Tom yanked the door open and forced her inside. "I've told you never to talk to strangers. What if they'd come to hurt you?"

"Why would anyone want to hurt her?" Violet asked.

He curled his lips into a snarl. "Don't tell me how to manage my wife. Get off my property. You've got no cause to be here." He marched to the edge of the porch, rage glowing in his eyes.

Violet inched back, her expression livid, presumably from Tom's declaration of "managing" his wife. "We came to see Mary Alice."

"Why?" he demanded. "She's not well, and you're harassing her. I ought to press charges."

Violet scoffed. "What kind of charges?"

"Harassment! For making her scream. For making her cry. She's not well, and you're scaring her."

"You're scaring her," Violet snapped back.

Wyatt pressed forward, mimicking Tom's movement and body language. He angled himself to shield Violet and Maggie from the lunatic on the porch. He'd had enough of Tom's yelling. "We didn't mean to upset her, Mr. Masterson. We only came because we know how close she and Violet's grandma are."

Mary Alice watched through the screen door, her palms pressed to the mesh on either side of her face. "I want to see her," she said. "I didn't know she was hurt. I don't understand what happened. I need to see she's okay."

"Shut up, Mary," Tom said, sounding tired.

"We don't know what happened, either," Violet said, stepping around Wyatt's shoulder, putting herself back in Tom's line of sight. "She's not okay."

Tom roared in frustration. He smacked the wall beside the front door, sending Mary Alice back a step. "Go sit down," he said. "She's an old lady who fell off a ladder. That's all."

"That's all?" Violet challenged.

Mary Alice's eyes brimmed with unshed tears as she returned to the screen, glaring at her husband.

"Yeah," he groused, "that's all."

Mary Alice spun away, slamming the front door behind her.

Tom braced his hands on his hips. He rolled his shoulders and widened his stance. "Come back here again, upsetting my sick wife, and I'll have a restraining order issued. Now, for the last time. Get. Off. My. Property."

Violet turned away, starting for Wyatt's truck in quick, easy strides.

Wyatt stared at Tom a while longer, assessing, challenging. Waiting to see if he'd blurt something useful in a fit of agitation.

He didn't.

"Have a nice day Mr. Masterson," Wyatt drawled, slow and intentional. "Probably be seeing you around soon."

Wyatt didn't know how or why, but he was sure Tom Sr. had something to hide. Wyatt's gut suggested it was something Tom would hurt anyone to keep covered. Violet's grandma. Ruth. Violet. A baby. Even his own wife if necessary.

Wyatt gave the Masterson home a long look as he pulled away, hoping Mary Alice didn't take any questionable falls before he figured things out.

Chapter Ten

Violet sipped iced tea and watched the dimming daylight from her grandma's back porch, thankful Wyatt had insisted on coming home before hurrying over to the hospital. She hadn't realized at the time how much the day's events had worn on her, but she felt it now, even all these hours later. She'd even fallen asleep sitting up at the kitchen table while Maggie took an afternoon nap. Violet smiled against the rim of her glass, enjoying the sight of Maggie on the porch at her feet, gnawing on her favorite plastic pony. She couldn't seem to decide which she enjoyed more, cuddling the bulbous pink horse or biting its head.

The back door opened and Wyatt appeared, filling the frame as he passed. "You ladies doing okay out here?"

Maggie stopped to smile a moment before going back to work on her pony's rounded ears.

Violet did her best to look at ease, though she doubted he'd believe the facade. Wyatt seemed to see past everyone's smoke and mirrors, his mind always at work, processing, evaluating. He studied people when they spoke, watched their hands as they moved. If only she'd had more insight when it came to love. She might not have spent the first half of her pregnancy crying tears of heartbreak over Maggie's father's rejection and the second half angry she'd been so stupid. She might've even known that he wouldn't matter at all once she saw Maggie's sweet face in that delivery room. After that, Maggie was the only thing that had mattered. She couldn't help wondering if Wyatt saw past all her other pretenses, too. Did he know the way her traitorous heart flipped and floundered at the sight of him, or the way he appeared in her fantasies? First the dirty ones, then lately, the ones about being a family?

Wyatt tilted his head, zeroing in on her in his trademark style, sending gooseflesh up her arms and coiling a spring in her stomach.

Violet cleared her throat. "Pull up a chair. There's a beautiful view, but it's going fast."

Wyatt lowered his large frame onto the porch beside Maggie and made a goofy face at her.

She squealed.

His cheek kicked up on one side. "I doubt this view ever goes bad."

Violet fought the blush warming her cheeks. Lines like those weren't helping her quest for clarity. "Any luck with your research?"

"No. I've put Sawyer on it, though, and he's excellent at finding things that others have tried to bury." He locked his jaw and averted his gaze. Frustrated? Violet tried and failed to read him the way he seemed to so easily read her.

"We can ask a few questions at the hospital," she suggested, wishing she had more to offer. "I wish I knew what Grandma had planned while you were here. I'd happily pick up the torch for her if I could find it."

Wyatt adjusted his long legs, bending one knee to his chest and dropping the opposite foot off the porch's edge. "You and me both."

Wyatt had spent the day hunched over his laptop, using his cell phone hot spot for internet service. He'd researched Henry Davis, the Masterson family and Violet's grandparents. So far, he hadn't found a clear link between the Mastersons, the Ameses and Mr. Davis. "I'd like to know what Mary Alice thinks she gave your grandma," he said. "She lost her mind when she thought it was lost, whatever it was."

"I know," Violet said. "I figure that's what the burglar tore the house up looking for, but I haven't seen anything unusual around here. Just Grandma's stuff and now a bunch of our luggage."

They needed Grandma. "Feel like going for a drive?" Violet asked.

"Hospital?"

"Yeah. I know someone would have called if anything had changed," Violet began.

"But you'd like to see her," Wyatt finished. "I don't blame you."

Maggie shoved her toy against his hand. "Po."

Wyatt raised a brow. "Pony?"

"No!"

Wyatt laughed. "Come on, short stuff." He pulled her into his arms and stood fluidly, then offered a free hand to Violet. "Might as well make that trip now and get as much as we can out of evening visiting hours."

"Thanks." Violet ignored the electricity climbing her arm to her chest as Wyatt pulled her onto her feet.

The hospital was quieter in the evening than it had been during Violet's previous morning visits. She supposed folks had already headed home for dinner by now. It was after seven and they'd be kicked off Grandma's floor at eight.

Violet veered across the hall to the nurses' station when she spotted Tanya's blond head tilted over a computer screen. "Excuse me, nurse?" she said sweetly.

Tanya lifted her face. "Yes?" Her smile doubled at the sight of Violet. "I hoped I'd see you tonight." She rounded the desk and pulled Violet into a hug. Her pale blue scrubs had tiny American flags on them. "How are you doing? I'm sorry I missed you yesterday. I'm covering so many shifts this week, I don't know which way is up."

"Don't forget to rest when you can," Violet warned.

"Always the mama," Tanya said. Her brows lifted. "Where is Maggie?"

Violet looked behind her. "There." She pointed across the wide hall where Wyatt was doubled over at the waist, gripping Maggie's tiny hands in his as she attempted to walk. Her dimpled arms stretched high over her head as she swung clumsy legs out before her.

Violet laughed softly. "She's barely managed to pull herself up," she told Tanya. "I think it's safe to say he's getting the cart before the horse over there."

"I could be training the next Ninja Warrior," Wyatt

said, clearly eavesdropping. "An Olympian, a professional bull rider or..." He swung her into his arms and made a gravely serious face. "What do you want to be when you grow up?"

She clapped and smiled proudly, showing off both of her new bottom teeth.

He headed for Violet and Tanya. "She's undecided. I don't think we should rush her."

Violet rolled her eyes, utterly enjoying Wyatt's ease and comfort with Maggie. "Wyatt, this is my cousin, Tanya. Tanya, this is Wyatt."

"Ah," Tanya said. "This is the boyfriend folks have been talking about."

"Nice to meet you," Wyatt said.

Tanya gave him a long once-over.

"Anything new with Grandma?" Violet asked, forcing Tanya's attention off of Wyatt's fantastic torso.

"No. Nothing, but the doctor thinks she's through the worst. He expects she'll be waking up soon. There's no physical reason that she wouldn't."

Violet's shoulders drooped in relief. "Really?"

"Yeah. It's just a matter of time now. Everything post-op looks really good. Grandma's strong, Violet," Tanya said. "She'll get through this, and she'll probably have one heck of a story to tell."

Violet's smile grew. "No doubt."

The desk phone began to ring and Tanya frowned. "I've got to get that, but I'm on shift until eleven, so don't worry about the posted visiting hours. I'm not about to kick you out." Her gaze turned back to Wyatt as she changed directions.

Violet felt a sliver of jealousy. Fake boyfriend or not, she was beginning to feel extremely, illogically, *stupidly* attached.

"Tanya?" Wyatt asked, stalling her cousin's retreat.

"Yes?"

"Do you know Mary Alice Masterson?"

"Sure. She's a good friend of Grandma's."

"How's she doing?" he continued. "We've heard she took a turn for the worse recently. Any idea what happened there?"

Tanya lifted a finger, then grabbed the phone long enough to put it on hold. "Mary Alice has been struggling for a long while," she told Wyatt. "She came in a few weeks ago after a fall in her kitchen. The doctors ran a bunch of tests that showed her dementia had significantly advanced. They recommended Mr. Masterson look at nearby assisted living facilities, but he was determined to keep her at home, so no one pushed."

Wyatt frowned. "He didn't have to take the doctor's advice? Do what was best for Mary Alice?"

"No. He's in good health and retired, so he can be with her all the time," Tanya said. "If her needs become too much, he can hire an in-home nurse or look into facilities then. Moving can be confusing for patients in Mary Alice's situation, and the transition can be tough. Each family has to make decisions based on their own timelines and abilities."

Wyatt's lids drooped. "Right."

Tanya smiled. "Sorry. I've got to take that call."

Violet leaned against his side. "Of course." She led the way to her grandma's room and settled into the chair beside her bed, then quietly whispered the story of everything she and Wyatt had seen, heard and experienced since she'd first received the call about her accident. Some people believed that coma patients were aware of the things going on around them. Violet hoped those people were right. "If you hear me, Grandma, I need you to wake up and tell me what all this means." She stroked hair off her grandma's forehead. "We need you," Violet whispered. "And I'm scared."

Wyatt's palm slid protectively over her shoulder, offering his peace and confidence.

Violet tipped her tear-dampened cheek against his finger, accepting the offer.

WYATT OPENED THE passenger door to his truck and waited as Violet fastened Maggie into the rear-facing car seat. Her dark curls were wild from static electricity. He waited while Violet climbed inside, then shut the door behind her. It had been a long day. One of many, but possibly his worst so far. Not knowing where Maggie had disappeared to this morning, then seeing her headed for a busy road… Wyatt's stomach fisted at the memory. A wave of nausea rolled through him as he climbed behind the wheel. He wasn't sure how Violet hadn't completely lost her mind. He could see the way it had worn on her, but she kept moving forward.

The silence in the truck was deafening. The night around them, suffocating. Violet's troubled expression reflected in the glass of her window.

"Want to talk about it?" he asked.

"I wish she'd wake up," Violet said. "Grandma's the

key to all this, whatever this is, and she needs to wake up." She fiddled with the fraying hem of her shorts. "I have a theory. Want to hear it?"

"Of course." He caught her gaze briefly before refocusing on the dark road.

Violet wet her lips and angled her body toward him in the shadows. "I think Mary Alice said something that didn't sit well with Grandma, so Grandma started asking questions. I think whatever it was bothered her so much she couldn't just let it go or chalk it up to Mary Alice's confusion and nothing more. And I think it has something to do with Henry Davis."

Wyatt couldn't disagree. Violet's idea was as good as any he'd had, but hers worried him. If Violet was right, it would be dangerous for her grandma to wake up. Whoever had hurt her before would likely be back to finish the job.

"And I think Mr. Masterson knows Mary Alice has a big secret," Violet went on. "I think her condition scares him because there's no way of knowing if she's forgotten it completely or if she's five seconds from announcing it to the mailman. He keeps her under his thumb so she doesn't tell, and the stress is getting to him. That's why he's drinking at eight in the morning, and that's why he wants me to go home."

"You think Mr. Masterson drove the derby car?" That was something Sawyer could research. Even if the car wasn't registered to Masterson, Sawyer could look at Masterson's local network, his friends and neighbors, and find the link if one existed.

"I do, and if I'm right, he knows he's in trouble. Either Grandma's going to wake up and take him down, or I'm going to uncover Mary Alice's secret while I'm looking for answers about what happened to Grandma."

"It's a solid theory," Wyatt said. "Maybe it's time we focus on the derby car. Find out who's behind the wheel, and we find out who wants you gone. Then we can figure out why." The car had no plates, but Wyatt had gotten a decent look at it as it sped away from the house. There had to be a register, photograph or something they could use to link the car to an owner.

"Thank you," Violet said. She sank straight white teeth into her bottom lip and turned wide blue eyes on him. "I'm glad you're here."

Wyatt forced his gaze back to the road. Remembering his place in her presence was harder all the time. He was too attached. Too attracted. He'd been hired by her grandmother to do a job, and so far he was failing. He'd gotten distracted playing house and entertaining ideas he hadn't had in a very long time. He wasn't husband or father material. If he ever had been, the military had carved it out of him. Even if he had heard the granite shell of his heart cracking when Maggie offered him her favorite pony. Even if Violet had trusted him to hold and comfort her. Even if he thought being loved by them might be all he needed to become the man he'd started out to be, it wouldn't matter if Violet didn't want another soldier in her life. Because no matter how long Wyatt lived or how many years eventually separated him from his active service days, he would forever be a ranger. There was no separating the two.

Blue and white flashers illuminated the darkness behind him, pulling him back to the moment.

"What?" Violet twisted and turned on her seat, craning for a look through the rear window. "Is that for you?"

"No." Wyatt eased his foot off the gas and drifted closer to the berm, providing the deputy with ample room to get around him on the winding country road. "I'm not speeding. I'll just get out of his way."

The cruiser stayed on his tail several seconds more, then added a siren to the flashers.

Violet scoffed.

Wyatt pulled over. He got out his driver's license and truck registration, then stacked them with his license to carry a concealed weapon. He powered his window down and waited. Fingers gripping the wheel at ten and two, he caught the cards between his fingertips.

"This is ridiculous," Violet complained. "They haven't done enough to scare and harass us? Now we're going to get run off the road or pulled over every time we get in a vehicle?"

A bright light hit the side of Wyatt's face and he grimaced. "Everything okay, Officer?"

Deputy Santos turned his light on Wyatt's hands. "Points for being prepared."

"What seems to be the problem?" Wyatt asked. "I'm sure I wasn't speeding."

Deputy Santos shone his light on the pieces of identification. "This is your truck?"

"Yes, sir. Bought it new the same month I was discharged."

"Any reason this truck might've been reported as stolen?"

Wyatt felt his jaw drop. He snapped it shut. "No, sir." Wyatt had worked damn hard for the money to buy this truck, and the vehicle had practically been his second home since opening Fortress Security. Yet someone had said he'd stolen it? His grip tightened on the wheel.

"Do you have a concealed weapon with you now?" Santos asked.

"Yes, sir. I've got a piece at my ankle and another in the glove box."

"Any reason for that? Two handguns seems like a little overkill for your average weekday evening."

"You'd think," Wyatt muttered. He locked eyes with the deputy, weighing a major decision. Had he been right about him? Was he a potential ally?

"He's protecting Maggie and me," Violet answered suddenly. She leaned across the bench for a better look at the deputy.

Santos shifted his weight, returning the IDs to Wyatt. "I'm glad you've got someone here to help you feel safe, Miss Ames. I'm just not sure this is a two-gun town." He worked up a smile, possibly an attempt to lighten the mood.

"That's not what I meant," she said.

Wyatt leaned over the door frame, making the decision to confide in someone who could possibly help them and hoping the quick background check he'd run on Santos revealed all he'd needed to know. "Okay, here it is. I'm not her boyfriend. I'm a personal security agent from Lexington, hired by her grandma just days before the woman took an unexpected fall that's put her in a coma. Now I'm here to find out what had her so scared that she felt she needed outside protection instead of just contacting the local sheriff and his crew."

Santos rocked back on his heels. He looked toward his car, then up the road before returning his attention to Wyatt. "Go on."

"You know as well as I do that in the few days since I came to town, Violet's been run off the road, I've been accused of harassment, my truck got a busted window, her car was scratched to hell with the clear message, 'go home.' The house has been burgled, her baby was set outside and left alone this morning near a road. We found her ten yards from a busy street, and now my truck has been reported as stolen. I've got reason to be extra cautious. It feels like a two-gun town to me."

Deputy Santos narrowed his eyes, then swore beneath his breath. "I'll contact dispatch, let them know the truck is clear."

"Thank you."

Santos rubbed his forehead. "I'll pull up the reports on Mrs. Ames's fall and see if anything seems off."

Wyatt tipped his hat in appreciation and the deputy was gone.

Violet watched as he drove away. "Do you think he'll tell anyone?"

"No, but we need someone in law enforcement who will stick up for us if we're right about the corruption." He eased onto the road and smiled at Violet, hoping to look more confident than he felt. "Try not to worry."

She peeked over her shoulder at Maggie, then settled back in her seat. "That's not going to happen."

Wyatt divided his attention between the road before him and the darkness reflected in his rearview. He pressed the gas pedal with a little more purpose. The sooner they were home, the better.

"Who do you think reported your truck stolen?" Violet asked. "Can anyone do something like that?"

"I don't know." His attention returned to his rearview.

Another car had pulled in behind them at the last crossroads, and the silhouette, though masked by the blinding headlights, looked a lot like another deputy's cruiser.

The blue and white lights began to spin on top before he could tell Violet to be prepared.

"You're kidding," she grumbled, twisting for a better look at the lights.

Wyatt pulled over, gathered his identification and put his hands where they were easily visible once more. "It's fine," he assured her. "We're less than a mile from your grandma's house. We'll head straight there from here and call it a night."

She crossed her arms and frowned. "This is ridiculous. How can they get away with this?"

"They're just doing their jobs."

"This is not okay," she said. "Someone lied to the sheriff's department for the sole purpose of causing you trouble."

Sheriff Masterson strode up to the window and sucked his teeth. "License and registration."

Wyatt handed him the papers he hadn't had time to put away since his last stop.

Sheriff Masterson glanced at them, uncaring. "You want to step out of the vehicle for me?"

"Sir." Wyatt spoke before touching his door handle. "I handed you my license to carry a concealed weapon, and I have a gun on my person."

The sheriff pulled his chin back and rested a palm on the butt of his sidearm. "Are you planning to use your weapon tonight, son?"

"No, sir."

"Then get out."

Wyatt cast a look in Violet's direction. "Be right back. Stay in the truck."

"Come on," the sheriff urged, impatient.

Wyatt moved to stand outside his truck, keeping a respectable distance from the sheriff. The air was warm and thick around them and filled with night sights and sounds. Stars, fireflies, owls and crickets.

No witnesses.

The sheriff stared. "I got a notice that this vehicle was stolen. You know anything about that?" He pointed his flashlight into Wyatt's eyes.

"Yes, sir. Your deputy just pulled me over for that five minutes ago. He read the registration I gave him. This is my truck."

The light moved away and Wyatt blinked furiously, bringing the sheriff back into view. His face was masked in a disbelieving look. "Are you giving me an attitude?"

"No, sir. I'm explaining."

"*Com*plaining sounds more like it," the sheriff said, cutting him off. "Do you have a problem I need to know about?"

Wyatt bit down hard on the insides of his cheeks. He couldn't let himself be baited. He needed to get Maggie and Violet to safety.

"I hear you visited my mother today," the sheriff continued. "How'd that go?"

Wyatt squelched a groan. The conversation had taken an ugly, and probably unavoidable, turn. "Not well."

Sheriff Masterson nodded. "My dad told me all about it when he called asking for a restraining order. You want to tell me what you were doing over there bothering my sick mama?"

"Violet and I were paying a respectful visit to her grandma's best friend. Nothing more. We thought she might want to be updated about what happened to Mrs. Ames."

The sheriff crossed his arms. "Dad says you made her cry. Seems to me you're a nuisance. A harbinger of trouble. Have you considered taking your vandal's advice and seeing your way back out of town?"

Violet's head and shoulders popped through the open driver's-side window. "We are not leaving town until we know my grandma's okay. Period. I don't care what else happens. You know," she seethed, "as far as sheriffs go, you're pretty horrible at your job."

Anger flashed in the sheriff's eyes, and he took a step toward Wyatt's truck. "You shut your face. No one asked you, you—"

Wyatt thrust himself between the sheriff and Violet. "Watch it now. You want to think before you finish that sentence." His blood boiled and his fingers curled into fists at his sides. "And you'd be best to find a respectful tone when you speak to her again."

The sheriff took a step back. He looked at Wyatt's steaming face, then at the fists, still clenched tightly on both sides. "Are you threatening me?" He reached for the cuffs on his belt and shook his head. "Threatening an officer gives me cause to haul you in."

"That's crap!" Violet said. "That's an abuse of power."

Wyatt turned to stare at her. He moved his head in a tiny warning. "Keys are in the ignition. Call Fortress. Talk to Sawyer. He can be here in an hour. Lock up tight until he gets here. Trust him when he does."

The cuffs pinched, cold and angry around Wyatt's wrists as Sheriff Masterson crammed them on, yanking each arm behind his back. He forced Wyatt to the cruiser, then pressed his face against the warm hood to pat him down. He removed the gun from Wyatt's ankle strap.

Sheriff Masterson clucked his tongue as he towed Wyatt upright. "I sure hope Miss Ames and that baby are going to be okay without you."

"Son of a—" Wyatt yanked himself around and towered over the sheriff. "You keep your hands off her."

"Another threat? You're on a roll tonight, huh, big guy?"

"If anything happens to either of them before I get out of these cuffs, I'm going to hold you personally responsible, and I won't care how long you want to lock me up when I'm done with you."

The sheriff's face was bloodless as he pushed him back. "Go on. Get in."

Wyatt dropped onto the cruiser's back seat, anger roiling in his chest. He nodded to Violet as the cruiser passed her window.

She pulled his truck into line behind them and took the turn toward her grandma's home.

Wyatt prayed Sawyer could get to River Gorge before the next bomb fell.

Chapter Eleven

Violet drove Wyatt's beast of a truck right onto Grandma's lawn, pulling as close to the front porch as possible before shifting into Park. She'd dialed Fortress Security while Sheriff Masterson had crammed Wyatt's face against the hood of his cruiser, then explained the night's events to Sawyer. The engine of his vehicle had growled through the line as she spoke.

Sawyer was on his way.

Still sitting in the truck, Violet noticed how the headlights flashed over ruined rows of Grandma's prized roses, and her heart lodged in her throat. The mulch was littered with red and white buds, pink petals and whole yellow flowers, all chopped and crushed into the ground. The remaining stems were headless, thorn-covered sticks, standing broken and naked in the moonlight.

It was a silly thing to care about in the big scheme of things. They were just flowers. Only plants. But it was *another* threat. And it hit home hard. Whoever had done this knew how important the roses were to her grandma. And it only solidified Violet's opinion that Mr. Masterson was the villain in this story. Not good news since she doubted his jerk of a son would ever arrest him, short of catching his father in the act of murder. Maybe not even then.

In the morning, Violet would talk to her grandma's doctors about moving her to a facility outside Grove County, somewhere the Mastersons couldn't reach her.

Anywhere but here.

Violet scanned the dark yard once more, thankful they'd left the porch light on. "One," she whispered, steadying her nerves and checking her rearview. "Two." She gripped the handle at her side. "Three." Violet popped the door open and jumped out. She flung the cab's back door open and hoisted Maggie's car seat from the cradle, baby and all. Then she shut both doors with the flick of a wrist and bump of a hip. They flew onto the porch in three long strides. Violet juggled her sleeping baby in the heavy car seat while trying to work the key into Grandma's new lock. Her clumsy hands and fraying nerves made the simple task nearly impossible.

"Come on," she scolded herself as fear crawled all over her.

The night sounds seemed to close in on her. The wind was an ominous whisper in her ear, a chill along her neck.

She wrenched the door open and slammed it shut behind her with a whimper, securing the dead bolt and chain before checking the other doors and windows. "All clear," she whispered to herself, repeating Wyatt's confident phrase. The home was all clear. And she and Maggie were alone.

Violet scrubbed a heavy hand against her quivering lips, then forced her feet into motion. She tucked Maggie safely into her crib, then returned to the first floor to put on a pot of coffee. Next, she lowered her grandpa's old rifle from its ornamental spot above the fireplace and loaded the heirloom with ammunition. Violet hadn't had any target practice in a decade, but if someone came close enough to hurt her or Maggie, she wouldn't miss.

Her mind raced, cluttered with the awful day's events. Losing Maggie at the library. Watching Wyatt be forced away from her. Her heart even ached for Grandma's roses. Violet had helped her choose the plants. She'd shoveled mulch and kept them watered each night as the sun went down. She'd tended them dutifully and with love until her last day in River Gorge. After that, she'd enjoyed Grandma's calls to her college dorm room, updating her on the blooms. She'd been ecstatic to learn Grandma had won prizes for them at the county fair, and she'd been honored when Grandma planted a bush of white roses in Maggie's honor following her baby's birth. That tribute had meant the world, and now those buds lay scattered among the mulch, angrily trampled by whoever had committed the crime.

Two mugs of coffee later, a set of headlights flashed over the front window, and Violet raised Grandpa's rifle. She marched slowly to the living room and peeled back the curtain. An old-model Jeep Wrangler sat in the drive behind her car. No driver.

She dropped the curtain and pressed her back to the wall, counting silently to settle her nerves, then she looked again. A man dressed in all black stood just outside the glass.

Violet clamped a hand over her mouth to keep from voicing her shock.

"Miss Ames." A slow Southern drawl slid under the door and around the window frame, smooth as molasses and warm as fried chicken. "I'm Sawyer Lance. You can put the weapon down. I believe you invited me here."

Violet stayed out of sight, but kept the rifle in clear view of the window. "Show me some ID."

The man positioned a small white rectangle in his fingertips and extended his arm toward the window. "Sawyer Lance," he repeated. "Fortress Security."

Violet peeked.

His hair was sandy and overgrown, his beard thick and unkempt. His fitted T-shirt and jeans gripped every muscular plane of his body. He wasn't as big as Wyatt, but he was close and twice as scary. The Fortress Security business card in his hand had his name embossed in black letters.

"Do you have a photo ID?"

He snorted, then bent at the waist peering through the glass, hands cupped at the sides of his face for a better view. "Are you kidding me?"

"Come on," she demanded, waving the rifle's barrel. "Show me, or get off my grandma's property."

He mumbled under his breath, then wrenched upright and fished a wallet from his back pocket. "I would like to state for the record that you're implying I'm not me, which means someone is out here impersonating me and in possession of my business card. Furthermore, you are suggesting someone has gotten the best of me, taken my cards and vehicle and left me behind." He turned a military ID in her direction. "I realize you do not yet know me, but trust me when I say that ain't ever gonna happen."

"Where's your driver's license?" she asked, stalling. Wyatt had told her to trust Sawyer, but opening the door to another stranger was proving tougher than she'd imagined.

"Expired while I was overseas."

Violet inhaled deeply and opened the door.

Sawyer walked in. He dropped a black duffel on the couch and scanned the room. "How many people in the house?"

"Two," Violet said. "My baby, Maggie, and me. Well, now you, too."

"How old's the baby?"

"Eight months."

He nodded. "You were right not to trust me. I could've been dangerous, but I'm not."

She felt her brow furrow. Her gaze lingered on his scarred face. The angry puckered skin of a newly healed burn marred the area over his left eye.

Pale blue irises studied her as she studied him. He kicked his cheeks up in a sudden grin. "I mean, I'm not dangerous to you, but I definitely am dangerous." He waltzed through the room, heading for the kitchen.

"Where's the baby? How many rooms on each floor? How many entrances and exits?"

Violet struggled for words and tried to keep up. She answered as many questions as she could while he checked her work, testing the door and window locks, then exploring the home in detail. "Why haven't you gotten a new driver's license?"

"I just got home. Newly discharged."

"How new?"

His smile dropped. "New enough. Where would you like me to set up for the night?"

"Wyatt slept on the couch."

"Sounds good to me."

Violet squirmed, the need to be hospitable warring with her desire to run upstairs and drag the bed in front of the door again. "I'll get you some coffee." She turned for the kitchen without waiting for a response.

Sawyer followed.

Violet's chest constricted as she poured two mugs, recalling the way Wyatt had done the same just hours before. Where was he now? Why hadn't he called? What was Sheriff Masterson doing to him? Would Wyatt have an "accident," too?

She rubbed her eyes as tears threatened to form.

"You must really hate coffee," Sawyer said.

She jerked her gaze to meet his. "I hate that Wyatt's stuck in jail when he didn't do anything wrong, and I don't know what's happening to him."

"He's fine." Sawyer set his mug aside and began unloading a laptop from his shoulder bag.

"How do you know? Have you spoken to him?"

Sawyer stopped to stare. "Have you met him? Trust me. He's fine."

She flopped onto a vinyl padded chair at her grandma's kitchen table and pinched the bridge of her nose.

"You guys are close?" Sawyer asked.

"He's the only person I trust," she said defensively, hoping Sawyer couldn't see straight through her, too.

"Well, I'm going to try not to take that personally," he said, logging on to the laptop and typing in a password. "Where's your Wi-Fi?"

"No Wi-Fi. Wyatt's using his phone as a hotspot."

"Great." The tone of his voice made it clear Sawyer didn't think that was great at all. He extended long, lean legs beneath the table and stretched his neck slowly, tipping his head over each shoulder.

The phone rang before Violet could tell him to suck it up. She strode to the wall and lifted the receiver. "Hello?"

"Violet Ames?" a man asked. "This is Roger at River Gorge General Hospital."

"Yes," she answered breathlessly. "This is Violet. What's happened? Is my grandmother okay?"

Sawyer stilled. His eyes lifted, focusing wholly on her.

"I'm sorry to say she's taken a turn for the worse. We're calling the family in now."

Her heart sputtered. "What?"

"You should probably make your way back here," he said. "I'm sorry."

Nausea rocked Violet's gut as she hung the receiver back on its cradle. "My grandma isn't going to make it," she said, barely believing the words. "We were just there. She was doing great." *Someone's done something to her.* Bile rose in her throat at the thought.

"I'm sorry to hear that." Sawyer slid a key ring across the table in her direction. "Take the Jeep. No one here will recognize it. I'll stay and watch over Mandy."

"Who?"

"The baby." He pointed up the staircase. "Your daughter."

"Maggie."

He nodded. "Unless you want to wake her. Then I'll just hold down the fort. Whatever you want."

Violet worked her mouth shut. She didn't want to wake Maggie or leave her with a man she'd just met who couldn't even remember her name. She also didn't want to take Maggie back out on the road when who knew where the next disaster would occur.

Wyatt's words echoed back to mind, strong and assured. *Lock up tight until he gets there. Trust him when he does.*

She turned her eyes back on Sawyer. He was a mess. Scarred face. Bruised knuckles. Messy hair, matted beard. He looked more like the problem than the solution, but Wyatt trusted him, and she trusted Wyatt. Violet took the keys from the table. "Maggie shouldn't wake up before dawn. Don't touch her if she does. Just call me on the number I called you from earlier. I'll be home in an hour. If I'm not, I'll be in touch again."

He gave her a limp salute.

"Keep her safe," she ordered.

"That I can do all day."

VIOLET RAN THE length of the empty second-floor hallway to the nurse's station. Tanya leaned against the desk, speaking to another nurse in patriotic scrubs. Her eyes widened at the sight of Violet.

"Sorry I took so long," Violet said. "Have they moved her? I just realized I don't even know if this is the right floor anymore." Was she in another ward now? Critical care or wherever patients go to… Her throat ached and she couldn't swallow. She worked to collect a full breath and some of her senses. "What can I do?"

Tanya looked as if Violet had grown a second head. "What are you talking about?"

"Grandma," Violet answered, frustrated and suddenly uneasy. "Someone called to tell me to get down here."

"Why?"

Violet's limbs went limp with confusion. "Something went wrong. The hospital was calling in the family."

"What went wrong?" Tanya asked. "Grandma's the same as she was when you were here before." Her eyes turned suspicious. "Who did you say called you?"

"Roger." Violet turned toward Grandma's room. "Roger from River Gorge General Hospital."

Tanya shook her head slowly in the negative. "I don't know anyone named Roger, and I've been here all night."

Violet burst into motion, racing for her grandma's room and praying that the phone call she'd received was a mean joke and not a threat on her grandma's life.

Her shoes skidded over the highly polished floor and ground to a halt outside her door. "Grandma?"

The curtain was pulled around the bed, making her grandma invisible in the dimly lit room.

"Grandma?" Violet's skin heated. Her stomach knotted. Her tongue seemed to swell in her mouth as she hit the light switch and dived for the drawn curtain. Terror seized her chest as she whipped the flimsy curtain back.

Grandma's face was serene and waxen as it had been during visiting hours, but the rolling tray used for mealtime had been positioned over her middle.

Tears stung Violet's eyes as she took in the gruesome message before her.

The tray's faux-wood finish was covered in crushed rosebuds and petals. A note lay among the destroyed blooms, stained with color from their petals.

Your baby or your grandma, Violet? You can't protect them both.

48 hours and the clock starts now.

Chapter Twelve

"Oh my goodness!" Tanya rushed in from the hallway and dashed to Violet's side. "Who did this?"

Violet spun on her. "Who was in here last?" She pulled her phone from her pocket and dialed Sawyer. He needed to check on Maggie immediately.

"No one," Tanya said. "I looked in on her when you left, then turned out the light and went on my rounds." She dragged worried eyes back to the roses. She lifted a shaky hand toward the note.

"Don't," Violet warned, shoving her hand away. "Don't touch it. There could be fingerprints there that will help us know who wrote it."

Tanya shoved her hands into her pockets and rocked back on her heels. "Why aren't you freaked out? What's going on? What aren't you telling me?"

Violet lifted a finger to indicate that she needed a minute, then she reported the incident to Sawyer and demanded he check on Maggie. Once she knew her baby was safe, she called the police. Dispatch took a report and promised to send a deputy, but Violet couldn't promise to wait. Her heart was being torn in two. She needed to be with Maggie, but Maggie had Sawyer, an armed, trained security agent and former army ranger. Grandma had Tanya, but someone had already gotten past her once. Though, to be fair, Violet hadn't been completely honest with her cousin about how much danger their grandma might be in. Maybe what she really needed to do now was confess. Coming clean with all the details might give Tanya an advantage, not put her at risk the way she feared. Maybe not knowing was the bigger risk.

She turned to Tanya. "We need to get Grandma out of here. She needs to be moved to a facility outside this county as soon as possible. I was coming to make the request first thing in the morning."

Tanya narrowed her eyes and crossed her arms. "Why?"

Violet weighed the notion. On the one hand, sharing details with Tanya could put her in danger. On the other hand, at least Tanya wasn't a baby or in a coma. She could help, and she deserved to know what was happening to their grandma. "I think someone connected to the sheriff's department, maybe even the sheriff or his dad, has been harassing me since I got here, and I think whoever is doing this is the same person who hurt Grandma."

Tanya's eyes widened. "She fell."

"Sure. After she was knocked down."

"Off a ladder," Tanya corrected.

Violet shook her head slowly in the negative. "And the man I was here with earlier isn't my boyfriend. He was hired by Grandma to protect her, but she didn't have a chance to tell him why. She was already here by the time he got to her place."

Tanya dragged her gaze from Violet to their grandma and back again.

Violet thought she saw an argument forming on her cousin's lips. Yes, everything she'd just said sounded crazy. It was crazy. And it was all true.

Tanya wobbled to the guest armchair and collapsed onto it. She slid her attention to the letter on Grandma's tray. A threat and a countdown. "Okay," she said. "I'll talk to the doctor first thing in the morning and tell him she needs to be closer to you because you're her preferred caregiver. Then I'll call every good facility in the neighboring counties to see which ones have a bed available."

Violet wrapped her in a quick hug. "Thank you." She stepped back with an apologetic frown. "I can't stay here and wait for the deputy. I need to get home to Maggie, and I think I might stop by the sheriff's department on my way. He might be corrupt or he might not, but the whole force can't be. Maybe making a scene down there will get an honest deputy's interest piqued."

She posed her phone over the bed and snapped a half dozen pictures of the gruesome floral scene, then moved the rolling tray as far as possible from her grandma.

"What should I do?" Tanya asked. "I don't want to leave her, but I'm the only one on the floor for another twenty-five minutes. I need to be at the desk."

"Call security," Violet said. "Get someone up here to sit with her until a deputy arrives, but don't let a deputy in here by himself. There's something off about this case and the sheriff's department. I've got no real proof. Just a lot of coincidence and intuition."

"Intuition." Tanya bobbed her head, clearly shocked by the night's turn of events and the metric ton of mess Violet had just dumped on her. "Honey, that's the best tool in any woman's arsenal, and it's good enough for me."

Violet passed the receiver to Tanya from the phone beside Grandma's bed, stretching the spiral cord across the distance. "Here. Call security, but don't leave until someone gets here to take your place and remember what I said about the sheriff's department."

Tanya accepted the receiver, then pressed a few buttons on the handset. "Be careful."

Violet hesitated. "Don't tell anyone what I just told you. Do your best to act as if I didn't."

Tanya nodded.

Violet took the stairs to the parking lot, unable to stand idly waiting for the elevator and unwilling to let her anger fizzle before unleashing it on whoever would listen at the sheriff's department. How many times did she and her family have to be threatened before the sheriff did something about it? How could she believe he wasn't involved when he didn't seem to care what was happening to her? Wasn't that his job?

She climbed into Sawyer's Jeep and mashed the gas pedal to the floor. She nearly leaped from the vehicle when she arrived at the sheriff's department, fully primed with adrenaline and a thirst for justice.

The front door was flung open beneath her heavy hands and she marched to the front desk. "I'm here to see Sheriff Masterson," she told the gray-haired woman staring back at her. "My name is Violet Ames, and I'm not leaving until I do."

"What's this about?" the lady asked.

A door opened nearby and both women turned to look.

The smug-looking sheriff walked out, trailed closely by a brooding Wyatt. The men slowed at the sight of Violet. Wyatt regained himself first, then closed the distance to her side. He slid his hands over hers and pulled her to him. "Thank you for coming so fast," he said loudly, then much more softly, "Let's go."

She stiffened. "No. Someone threatened Maggie and Grandma. *Again.* My *baby* and *comatose* grandma," she seethed. "I came to talk to the sheriff." Her voice grew louder with each word, and several faces turned in her direction.

Sheriff Masterson went to stand with the gray-haired lady on the other side of the desk. "Is there a problem, Miss Ames?"

"Yes," she barked, drawing more attention as planned. "Someone in your town has repeatedly threatened and endangered my baby, my grandma and myself." She faced the screen of her phone to him and flipped through the photos taken at the hospital.

His jaw locked.

"What are you going to do about it?" Violet demanded. "She can't exactly leave town like you keep suggesting I do, now can she?" *Barring that hospital transfer I just requested.* Violet's nose and eyes stung with barely tamped-down emotion. The week's buildup was quickly reaching a tipping point, but she couldn't afford to look weak. She needed the sheriff to see her as strong. Unwavering. She steadied her breathing and plowed ahead. "And what kind of policy is that anyway? Anyone having trouble ought to just leave town? Then you can boast about how safe your county is? No crime here."

Wyatt pulled her against him and buried his face in her hair. "We need to go." He lifted his mouth to her ear. "Now."

Violet's will wavered. Wyatt's warm breath on the delicate skin of her neck and cheek had distracted her, defused her. She grimaced at the sheriff. "You need to help me. Help my grandma." She cast her gaze to all the other men and women in uniform watching her mental breakdown. "We have forty-eight hours."

She turned and let Wyatt lead her away.

WYATT STARTED SAWYER'S Jeep as Violet buckled in. "It was smart of you to take this vehicle. No one knows to look for you in it, and Sawyer keeps his glass tinted to the legal limits. This time of night, it'd be impossible to know who was driving."

Violet wrapped her arms around herself tightly and stared at the sheriff's department as they passed through the lot. "What happened in there?"

"Nothing. They left me in a room alone the whole

time. By the time I got a young deputy to allow me my phone call, they let me go. I called Sawyer, but pretended I was speaking with a lawyer."

She frowned. "You called Sawyer? Not me?"

"You were supposed to be with Sawyer. When he told me you were at the hospital, I thought I was going to have to walk there."

Violet rolled her eyes. "That's five miles away."

Wyatt eased onto the road and hooked a right toward Mrs. Ames's house. "So? You were there, and it's not like Sawyer could come and pick me up. He said he was instructed not to touch the baby, and he didn't have the keys to my truck anyway."

She looked his way. "So the sheriff hauled you all the way to the department just to leave you in a room and do nothing? No threats or grand inquisition? Nothing? What was the point?"

"Because he can?" Wyatt guessed. He'd assumed it was a typical bully's lesson. He's in power, so Wyatt must concede. He'd also considered it might be another warning.

"Did you see the photos I showed Sheriff Masterson?" Violet asked.

"Yeah." Wyatt caught her eye then. "It wasn't the sheriff. He never left the station. I could hear his big mouth in every room for almost two hours. Giving orders. Making stupid jokes. Watching a game on television in the break room. He didn't have time to get to the hospital after taking me in."

Violet let her eyes drift shut, then turned her face

away. "Maybe he pulled us over on his way from the hospital."

"Maybe, but we were also on our way from the hospital, so he would've had to be fast with the note and roses."

She pressed the heels of her hands against her eyes.

"We will find out who did this," Wyatt vowed. "I know I've said it before, but it's true, and I need you to trust me."

Violet's lips twitched, but the smile never formed. "The monster ruined her rosebushes."

"I'm sorry." The photos had been tough to see, especially the note. The devastation in Violet's eyes had sliced straight through him. "Those were her roses left at the hospital?"

She nodded, eyes glossy with unshed tears.

Wyatt reached out and pulled her as close as the seat belts would allow, then gripped her small hands in one of his and squeezed with promise. He released her when he pulled into her grandma's drive. The Jeep's headlights washed over the destroyed rosebushes and Violet's tiny car. The little yellow hatchback sat at an awkward angle. The two tires farthest from the house had been slashed, probably with whatever had been used to destroy the roses. "You didn't tell me about your car. I think it's having as rough a week as you are."

Violet wrenched upright and clamped her hands onto the dashboard. "I didn't even notice that earlier. I've barely looked at my car since it was carved up." She pounded her foot against the floorboard. "As if the paint job wasn't going to break the bank, now I need two new tires."

Wyatt forced a tight smile. "Maybe if you leave it sitting out here long enough someone will just take it and your car insurance will replace it with a whole new one." He met her outside the passenger door and walked her to the porch, maneuvering around his truck in the front yard. "Were you drunk when you parked my truck like that?"

"No."

She laughed, and the hardened shell of Wyatt's heart cracked a little further. "Well, you might consider retaking the parking test, 'cause you missed the driveway by about twenty-five feet."

She laughed again, this time taking his elbow in her hand as they climbed the steps.

Wyatt stopped short of opening the door, knowing it was the last time they'd be alone before he faced Sawyer and a long night of research. "Come here." He pulled Violet to his chest and wrapped her in his arms. To his great pleasure, she hugged him back.

More than that, she melded herself against him.

Wyatt's heart thundered and his hands slid over her narrow back, and he enjoyed the feel of her more than was remotely acceptable for their situation. He pressed one palm to the curve of her spine, fingers splayed over the thin material of her shirt, and drifted the other into the plane between her shoulder blades. "I'm sorry I wasn't with you at the hospital tonight." His voice was low and thick. Guilt had nearly consumed him as he'd sat in the empty room wondering if she and Maggie had made it home safely. "I'd promised to stay with you, to protect you. Instead, I let that menace bait me into saying the wrong thing."

"You were defending me," she whispered, turning her beautiful face up to his. "I was honored."

Wyatt pursed his lips. "I was stupid. Impetuous. I should've found another way to make him back off without causing us to be separated. If something had happened to you or Maggie..." The words stopped coming. He couldn't bear to finish the sentence.

Wyatt moved one palm to cup Violet's jaw. He let the pad of his thumb caress her cheek. Logically, he knew what he was doing was wrong and unprofessional and that she should tell him where to stick his grabby hands, but the look in her eyes was electric and the magnitude of that pull was enough to make him brave. Wyatt lowered his head. Closer. Breathing her in and waiting for the will to knock it off. This wasn't the job. And he wasn't that guy who'd take advantage of a stressed-out single mom who probably just wanted something safe and normal to hold onto amid all the danger surrounding her this week.

Violet rose onto her toes, arching her back and trailing her small hands over the curves of his chest to his shoulders. The unmistakable heat of desire darkened her eyes.

A low, needy moan rumbled through him as his nose lined up beside hers, seeking, testing. Tasting her sweet breath as it washed over him. Feeling the heat of her body pressed to his.

Her mouth was *right* there, waiting to be taken by him.

The home's front door swung open beside them and Violet sprang from his hold.

Sawyer stared out. "I heard you pull up like ten minutes ago. What are y'all doing out here? Is this a private discussion or are you about ready to get in here so we can get to work?"

Violet hung her head and darted inside, hiding her pink cheeks behind long brown hair.

Wyatt took a minute to pull his thoughts together and remind himself that he loved Sawyer, and he didn't really want to knock him out right now. "Thanks for coming."

"Anytime." Sawyer locked the door behind Wyatt, then followed him into the kitchen.

Violet was already at the table, hands folded and looking mighty guilty. Wyatt tried not to think too long or hard about why. "Did Maggie wake while I was away?" she asked.

"Nope." Sawyer dropped onto the chair positioned at the end of the table. "But she shouted, 'No!' so loud I thought someone had gotten in through an upstairs window. I was halfway to her room when I heard her snoring."

Wyatt grinned. That chubby-cheeked princess was a riot. He could imagine Sawyer ready for battle, tearing up the steps to defend the baby, only to see she was telling someone off in her dreams. *Probably me*, he thought wryly.

"That was about all I heard from her," Sawyer said.

"What about you, Stone?" he asked Wyatt. "How was jail?"

"Super."

Violet tapped her phone's screen as the men spoke. A moment later, she set the device aside. Both men's cell phones buzzed. "I sent you copies of the photos I took at the hospital. Just in case the scene goes missing. I have proof. Tanya saw it, too. What should we do now?"

Sawyer flipped through the photos. "Are these the roses from right outside?"

"I think so," Violet answered. "Some jerk was real busy tonight."

Wyatt itched to go to her, to comfort her. Would she really have let him kiss her? Did she want him to? And had he seriously not jumped on that opportunity? He felt his brows pull together. It had been the right thing to do. Hadn't it? It would have been wrong to let her confuse her appreciation for his protection with real feelings for him. Right?

Sawyer dropped his phone on the tabletop and shot a pointed look at Wyatt. "Small-town cover-up?"

"Yeah. Seems that way. Problem is going to be finding out who is covering for who. Binds run deep and tight in a town this small."

Sawyer expelled a long puff of air. "Nothing truer than that, and the way I understand it, your main suspect is the former sheriff." He rocked his chair back on two legs. "That's no good."

"Nope," Wyatt agreed.

"And that guy is the current sheriff's daddy, yeah?"

"Yeah."

Sawyer performed a long, slow whistle. "Doesn't get tighter than that."

No, it didn't. Wyatt shifted in his seat. "The cover-up theory is only a theory. We have no idea what's been covered up or why. Not even a guess."

Sawyer set his chair down with a thud. "Violet's grandma needed protection for some reason. Now her granddaughter and great-granddaughter do, too. Are you thinking this all started with something big?"

Wyatt nodded. "I doubt anyone would bother trying to run folks out of town over something small."

Sawyer did another whistle. A short, slick burst this time.

Violet rolled her head over one shoulder and fixed her gaze on Sawyer. "Any chance you've got some new information on Henry Davis?"

He tapped his pointer fingers along the worn Formica tabletop like drumsticks. "I'm working on it."

"What about the derby car?" Wyatt asked.

"Still working."

Wyatt scraped his chair back and went to the refrigerator for a bottle of water. "I'd like to know what kind of thing would motivate a person to threaten an old woman and a baby." Just the thought made his blood boil. He pressed the cold bottle to his forehead, then against the curve of his neck. "It's got to be something huge. Theft? Embezzlement? Gambling debt?"

"Why does it have to be about money?" Violet asked. "Maybe it's a case of identity theft or fraud. Maybe Sheriff Masterson helped Henry Davis disappear when he didn't want to go back to war, and Mary Alice's dementia makes it likely she'll forget that was a secret."

Sawyer stroked his ratty beard. "Maybe the sheriff isn't really a Masterson. Maybe the missing soldier is really his daddy and that kind of truth come to light would besmirch the family name."

"Besmirch?" Wyatt asked. "Really?"

"Hey, I know things," Sawyer said.

Wyatt smiled.

Violet flipped through the photos on her phone. "That note said I have forty-eight hours. I don't have any reason to think this will be sorted by then, so I told Tanya I want to move Grandma out of the county."

The men turned to face her. Neither spoke.

"Tanya said she'd talk to the doctor first thing tomorrow morning, then reach out to some facilities in search of an open bed. The note-writer was right. I can't protect them both. Unless Maggie and I move into Grandma's room at the hospital, I can't be in two places all the time. Maybe moving her into another county and putting her safety in the hands of another police or sheriff's department will help remove some of the danger."

Sawyer tented his brows. "Good idea."

Wyatt agreed with the move. Mrs. Ames would be safer somewhere outside the potentially corrupt sheriff's jurisdiction, but Wyatt wasn't so sure about Violet and Maggie. "I think you should stick with us until we know who's behind this. Going off on your own could be dangerous like we talked about." As long as he didn't do anything else to get himself hauled off to jail again, he'd never let Violet or Maggie out of his sight.

Violet yawned. "Let's see what Tanya has to say after breakfast." She rubbed her eyes. "I can try talking with Mary Alice again tomorrow."

Wyatt moved to stand beside her chair. "I don't know. I've heard the words *restraining order* more times than I'd like today. I think we'd be wise not to push the old man." He gave his partner a long look. "Maybe you can give Mary Alice a shot. No one knows you yet. Maybe take a walk down her street, see if you see a nice old lady on the gray-and-black craftsman-style porch with the American flag."

Sawyer smiled. "Ask her about the missing man from five decades back? Sounds good."

Violet yawned again.

Wyatt offered her his hand. "How about we move this to the living room? It's more comfortable in there, and I've already seen you fall asleep at this table today. Why not mix it up a little?"

Sawyer chuckled. "You're still a thrill a minute, I see."

Violet accepted his hand, then leaned against his side as they made their way back to the front room. She settled on the love seat and tucked her feet beneath her. Wyatt took the cushion on her right.

Sawyer sat on the floor, back resting against the couch, a clear view of the front window and door on one side, the hallway, kitchen and rear exit on the other. Wyatt knew because he'd spent his recent nights seated there, too, pushing the same few seemingly useless puzzle pieces around in his head.

Mary Alice, Mr. Masterson, a missing GI from 1968 and Violet's grandma.

In other words, a dementia patient, a drunk, a missing person and an old lady in a coma.

Basically, they had nothing and less than forty-eight hours to find out who'd written that note.

The clock was ticking.

Chapter Thirteen

Wyatt's eyes snapped open. He'd fallen asleep talking to Sawyer, trading theories and exploring the difficulties of investigation in a small town where the sheriff was angry and shady. He woke to the muted thuds of wood on wood. The warbled words of a voice on the morning air.

Sawyer rose to his feet across from him and crept down the hallway toward Mrs. Ames's kitchen. He'd heard it, too.

Wyatt blinked, forcing his eyes into focus. His mind had fixed on a distant sound.

The back door opened and shut softly.

Wyatt eased away from Violet. She'd tipped against him during the night, set her cheek on his shoulder and an open palm on his chest. "Shh," he soothed, detangling their warm bodies.

Violet's eyes cracked open, her expression mired in sleep. "Where are you going? Is it Maggie?"

"No." Wyatt stretched to his feet and collected his sidearm and holster from the table, securing them to his belt. "She's asleep. Stay here."

The sound came again, this time followed by a whistle.

Violet scooted to the edge of her cushion. "What was that sound?"

"Sawyer went to see. That was him whistling."

Her blue eyes cleared immediately. "A warning?"

"Nah," Wyatt said. "That whistle is more like, get out here and see."

"I'll get Maggie."

They parted ways in the kitchen, Violet taking the steps to the second floor and Wyatt moving through the back door and into the yard beyond.

Sawyer stood just inside the barn where Mrs. Ames had fallen, both hands on his hips. He nodded at the loft above. "There's our noisemaker. What do you suppose that's about?"

Wyatt stepped forward, peering into the cavernous structure, drawn to the continued thuds and murmuring. "Hello?"

Sawyer joined him, arms crossed. "Wonder how long she's been up there."

"She?" Wyatt asked.

"The old lady."

The loft boards rattled and Mary Alice appeared, pacing closer and closer to the edge. "Where is it?" she asked. "Where is it? Where did you put it? Where did it go?"

"Mrs. Masterson?" Wyatt asked, drawing her attention to the barn floor below. "What are you doing up there? Be careful. You're at the edge. Step back." Faint rays of amber-and-gold light filtered through the space between boards. Tufts of hay fell from the loft.

Wyatt craned his neck for a better look at the uninvited guest. "On second thought, why don't you come on down here and tell me how I can help?"

"Not until I find it!" she yelled. Her features hardened in a look of sheer defiance. "Where is it?" She spun away from the edge, but slid on the loose hay and stumbled. Her arms flew wide, grasping at air. "Oh!"

Wyatt shot forward, racing to the place where she would land if she fell. "Be careful!"

Mary Alice regained her balance and stared down at him through the space between loft boards. "Who are you?" she asked. "Why are you here?"

"I'm Wyatt Stone. A friend of Mrs. Ames. I'm here to help you."

Mary Alice stilled. Her ruddy cheeks went white. She tipped precariously forward, lowering her nose toward the boards at her feet. "Did she tell you about him?"

"Yes," Wyatt lied. "She trusted me with the truth. You can, too."

She straightened then, shuffling back from the edge. She pressed narrow, wrinkled hands over her mouth and sobbed. "I'm so sorry."

Maggie's sweet babbles reached Wyatt's ears before Violet made it into the barn. "What's happening?" Violet asked, moving into place between Wyatt and Sawyer.

"There's an old lady crying in your loft," Sawyer explained.

"Why?"

Sawyer pointed a silent finger at Wyatt.

"It's Mary Alice," Wyatt explained. "She's looking for *it*."

Violet stepped back, one hand against her forehead, seeking the woman overhead. "Mary Alice? Are you okay?"

Dust sifted through the boards overhead, fluttering to the earthen floor. "Gladys?" Mary Alice inched closer, her eyes puffy from tears. "Is that you?"

Violet frowned. "Does Tom know you're here?"

"No." She shook her head vigorously. "Of course not. You know I'm not supposed to leave."

Wyatt rubbed a hand through his hair. "I've got to call the sheriff's department. She's clearly confused, and her husband's probably worried." Much as he'd like to take advantage of having the woman alone for questioning, it wasn't right. She needed help he couldn't begin to give.

"Or he's drunk again," Violet grouched. "How about you call the sheriff, and I'll talk to Mary Alice? Maybe this is a blessing in disguise. I'd hoped to speak with her again."

Wyatt turned away, dialing the department. "Good luck. You'll probably only have about five minutes once I make the report."

"What?" Mary Alice called. "What are you saying, Gladys? Did you tell him? Did you tell that man about Henry?"

"Of course not," Violet said.

Wyatt darted forward, hoping to salvage the lie. "It's okay. I've already told her you trust me and she can, too."

Violet puckered her brow. "Oh."

"Liars," Mary Alice cried. "Everyone lies. I lie," she said. "I've lied all my life. I don't want to anymore."

Violet struggled with a wiggly Maggie, who'd nearly turned herself upside down trying to get to the floor. "It's okay," she promised. "I don't blame you. You can always talk to me when things get hard."

Wyatt finished his call and pulled Maggie into his arms. He tipped his head toward Mary Alice. "Keep going," he told Violet. "I've got princess."

She wet her lips and moved toward the ladder. "I'm sorry you're upset, Mary Alice. I never meant to upset you."

"You shouldn't have told," she said. "It wasn't your story to tell. I want the box back now."

"Okay." Violet turned victorious eyes on Wyatt. "What box?"

He motioned with one hand. "Keep going," he whispered.

Mary Alice didn't respond.

Violet reached for the ladder. "Can I come up? We can talk privately."

Wyatt cringed. That wasn't what he'd meant. He swept a hand out to stop her and missed.

Her fingers curled around the wood.

"No!" Mary Alice screamed.

Violet jumped back, rushing toward the center of the barn where Wyatt stood, looking up as Mary Alice continued to scream. "Sorry! I won't come up. I'll stay right here."

Mary Alice gave Wyatt a long questioning look.

"Are you here to arrest me?" she asked. Her gaze stuck to the sidearm on his hip.

"No, ma'am. I'm not here to arrest you." He cocked his head and trod lightly. "Why would I do that?"

"Because I kept his things," she said. "Hid them. Then gave them to Gladys, and now they're gone."

"They're in the box you're looking for?" he asked.

Mary Alice moved into view at the loft's edge then crumpled to the loft floor. "Yes." Her housecoat puddled around her as she lay in the hay, as if she'd disintegrated before his eyes and the ugly brown material was all that remained.

"Who do the things in the box belong to?" Violet asked.

"Mary Alice!" Mr. Masterson's voice boomed in the distance.

Wyatt spun in place. Shock and curiosity rushed in his mind.

Had someone from the sheriff's department told Mary Alice's husband where she was, or had he already been on his way looking for her? If so, then why had he assumed she would be here? Did he know that his wife had given Mrs. Ames something to keep for her?

The distant cry of a siren crept into the barn with them. Backup was coming, and Wyatt was willing to bet the first cruiser on the scene would be driven by the sheriff, Mary Alice's son.

Mr. Masterson plodded through the open barn door. His shadow stretched ominously before him. "Where is she? What did you do to her?"

Mary Alice sat up, revealing herself. "Here I am,"

she croaked, running the sleeve of her housecoat under her nose. Her sullen expression was caught somewhere between desperation and hopelessness. "Take me home."

Mr. Masterson stomped into the room's center. His blue T-shirt was untucked, and his blue jeans needed a belt. He hadn't tied his boots or combed his hair, and the heady scent of beer lingered on his breath. "Get down here. What are you doing up there? You know you aren't supposed to leave."

She swung trembling legs over the loft's edge and shimmied on her stomach, searching blindly for footholds on the creaky ladder. "I'm sorry. I didn't mean to."

"You didn't mean to walk out the front door while I was sleeping?" he groused. "Didn't mean to walk all the way over here without telling anyone? You didn't mean to climb into that loft? Didn't mean to scare me half to death? To defy my rules?"

Mary Alice began to cry again. She stopped her descent, her frail body jackknifed over the loft's edge.

"Easy," Wyatt warned both Mastersons. "Mary Alice, please take your time and be careful coming down. Mr. Masterson, watch yourself. I'm getting a good idea of how you treat your wife privately, and it isn't going to fly here."

"Is that a threat?"

Wyatt crossed his arms and squared his shoulders in answer.

Mr. Masterson scoffed. "I've got dogs who know

better than to push me. Are you smarter than my dogs, son?"

Wyatt bit the insides of his cheeks. The metallic taste of blood filled his mouth, pulling him back from the edge of saying something that might land him back in jail. He couldn't afford to give the sheriff a reason to take him away again, and threatening the man's father seemed a sure way to do exactly that.

The arriving siren peaked, then silenced outside the barn. The sheriff strode into the tension moments later, evaluating the scene before rushing to his mom's aid on the ladder. He whispered to her, calming her and helping her slowly to the ground. He lifted furious eyes to his father. "Dad? You want to explain to me what the hell happened here?"

Mr. Masterson stared at Wyatt, teeth gritted.

"I'm sorry," Mary Alice said. "I was only looking for his things."

"Whose?" Wyatt repeated his earlier question.

"Henry's." She cupped a hand over her lips and flipped her gaze to meet her husband's. "I think I should lie down."

"I think you should shut up," he muttered, ripping her roughly from their son's hands. "Let's go."

The sheriff followed closely behind his parents, looking more like a sullen boy than a man in charge of an entire county's safety.

Wyatt shadowed them, both sickened and aghast at the twisted family dynamic he'd watched play out.

"I shouldn't have kept his things," Mary Alice whispered loudly as they approached her husband's truck.

"I just wanted to return them to his people. It's the right thing to do."

"Shut. Up!" Mr. Masterson stopped and gave her arm a firm tug. His eyes were bright with rage.

"Dad," the sheriff warned.

Mary Alice whimpered and jerked away.

Mr. Masterson wrenched the passenger door open and nearly tossed her inside.

"Where are we going?" she asked, fumbling to right herself on the bench. "To the well?"

Mr. Masterson slammed the door. His eyes slid shut for a long beat.

The well meant something to him. But what?

His son closed in on him. "I'm heading to your place from here. I won't be ten minutes behind you."

Mr. Masterson climbed behind the wheel without another word and reversed down the drive.

Violet slid into place at Wyatt's side, tucking Maggie safely between them. "That was all kinds of disturbing," she said softly.

Sheriff Masterson turned to gawk, as if he'd somehow heard her. He tipped his hat and scowled. "Take good care of your grandma, Miss Ames. Ladies get old and bad things start to happen."

VIOLET'S HEART THUDDED roughly in her chest. Had the county sheriff just threatened her grandmother? In front of witnesses? Was he insane? She set Maggie in the grass with trembling hands, then dialed Tanya's cell phone, praying her cousin was at the hospital.

"Hello?" Tanya answered.

"How's Grandma?" Violet blurted. "Is security still with her? Have you spoken with the doctor?"

"Violet?" Tanya asked. "Are you okay?"

"I'm fine. A little shaken, but how's Grandma?"

"She's fine. There hasn't been any change."

"And the doctor?" Violet pressed.

"He hasn't been to this floor yet, but it's still early, and he's got patients on floors one and five, as well. I'll call as soon as I know more about the transfer. Okay? Right now, I need to make my rounds."

"What about security?"

"There's a man outside her door now. A new one will come when the shift changes."

Violet breathed a little easier. "Okay. Tell me as soon as you talk to the doctor about Grandma's transfer." She disconnected and turned to Wyatt, who'd swept Maggie off the ground when she'd crawled straight to him. "What was the name of that body shop you took your truck to?"

"R.G. Auto Body."

Violet tried to focus on the larger problem and not on the fact that her baby was getting too attached to a man who would soon be gone. "I want to get my tires replaced. I want to know Maggie and I can leave if we need to."

Wyatt shared the number, then played with Maggie while Violet made arrangements to have her car towed to the shop.

She wasn't sure if River Gorge was safe or if it was better for her to just go home to Winchester, but one thing had become abundantly clear. Violet needed a way to get Maggie out of town in case of emergency. She needed an escape plan, and a car with two bad tires wasn't going to get the job done.

Violet paid the tow truck driver when he came for her car, then went inside to check on Maggie and the guys.

Wyatt moved away from the window where he'd been watching her and went to stare over Sawyer's shoulder at a series of topographical maps spread over the kitchen table. Maggie's body was limp in his arms. Her head was cocked back. Her eyes closed in slumber.

Violet slipped in close and removed her baby from Wyatt's strong arms. "I'll put her to bed, then be right back."

"Take your time," he said.

Sawyer grunted, a pen between his teeth.

Violet slipped upstairs and tucked Maggie into her crib, then nearly leaped back down to see what they were doing with those maps. "What are the red marks for?" she asked. Had something happened while she was outside making arrangements to get her broken car fixed? "Are those local maps? River Gorge? Grove County?"

"Wells," Sawyer answered.

Violet dragged her attention from Sawyer to the maps, then fixed it on Wyatt. "What?"

"Mary Alice asked her husband where they were going in such a hurry. She asked if they were going to the well, and Mr. Masterson nearly stroked out in response."

"Everyone in town has a well," Violet said. "What are the maps for?"

"Everyone has a well," Wyatt said, "but they don't go to them. They are a resource, not a destination."

Sawyer spun a map in her direction. The page was marked over with blue ink. "The circles represent abandoned wells in this county. Some have probably been decommissioned by the state. The rest should be boarded over, but accessible. I'm going to pay them all a visit once I finish mapping them."

Violet turned the page back to face him. "There must be dozens. These marks are spread all over the county, and some of them are in the middle of nowhere. How will you even get there?"

Sawyer lifted one foot off the ground and gave it a wiggle.

Violet rolled her eyes. "That will take forever. I only have thirty-six hours."

"I'll drive to as many as possible, then hike to the rest."

Violet fought the frustration knotting in her muscles. It was all anyone could do. More than most, and Sawyer was ready. She needed to hope it was enough. "I need some fresh air."

Wyatt opened the back door for her as she passed. "Feel like taking a walk?"

Desperately. Violet pursed her lips. "I don't know. I just put Maggie down."

"I've got her," Sawyer said. "Babies love me. Especially Mandy."

"Maggie," Wyatt and Violet corrected in near unison.

Sawyer laughed. "I'm just yanking your chains. Go walk. Let me work."

Violet pulled in a deep breath, then grabbed the quilt off the back porch's swing on her way down the steps.

Wyatt fell into stride beside her with two bottles of water in one big hand. He offered one to Violet, then took the quilt from her and tossed it over his shoulder.

"Thanks." Violet accepted the water, then slid her free hand around his elbow as they walked.

Wyatt turned a careful smile on her. "We got off to a rough start this morning, but it's been a good day. Mary Alice said the box of things she's looking for belonged to Henry."

"She had to mean Henry Davis," Violet said. "There's no way there's a second Henry in this mess."

"I assumed as much, given your grandma's internet searches, and now we know the Mastersons visit a local well for some reason. Based on Mary Alice's tone, it's not a good time when they do. If we're lucky, Sawyer will find the well she was referring to, maybe even find the box and get this mess wrapped up by nightfall. Then that note won't matter. We'll know who wrote it before the forty-eight hours is up."

"It's a lot of wells."

"We've already got a plan in place, so he won't need to search them all. He'll be methodical and efficient with the ones he does."

Violet's mind raced as the torrent of emotions whipped through her. Fear for herself and her family. Sadness for Mary Alice and hers. Hope that this new revelation would be the one to break the case. And something else. Something warm and strange and new when she thought about the way her hand felt on Wyatt's strong arm, or the way he'd held her on the porch last night. For a moment, she thought he might want to kiss her, too.

Violet had sworn she'd never date another military man. Her ex had pridefully put service to his country above everything else, and when he learned he was having a baby, he'd dropped her like the plague. As far as she knew, he was still proudly serving his country. Her heart still stung for Maggie's sake. Violet knew what it was like to not know her father. It stunk. But maybe her ex was the exception and not the rule. Maybe all her fears of being hurt again, of seeing Maggie lose another male figure in her life, were keeping her from taking a chance on something amazing.

She glanced his way and caught him staring.

Or maybe she was a silly-hearted dreamer who wanted impossible things. Like a real, true, toe-curling, ballad-worthy love.

Wyatt slowed at the sight of the lake beyond Grandma's field. "Is this where we're headed?"

She cleared her throat and nodded. "Yeah." She hadn't really had a plan when she'd walked out the back door, but the lake was a good place to be still and think. Behind them, her grandma's barn and home were distant red and white dots. Had they really walked so far already?

Wyatt spread the quilt on the ground.

Violet lowered herself onto it, enjoying the mix of sun and shade as a warm breeze jostled the limbs of a mighty oak overhead.

Wyatt took a seat beside her, his brown eyes searching. "I'm glad Sawyer's here," he said finally.

She smiled. She wasn't sure what he'd been going to say, but she hadn't considered that Sawyer would have anything to do with the conflict wrinkling his brow. "Oh yeah?"

Wyatt reached for her hand and pressed his palm to hers, twining their fingers and looking as guilty as any man she'd ever seen. "I'm glad he's here because I've let myself become distracted. I've gotten too involved and become too emotional to do the job I need to do."

Violet rolled her eyes, trying not to overthink the meaning behind his words. "Yeah. You seem like a real wreck."

"I am." Wyatt pulled their joined hands to his chest, soulful eyes still searching hers. "I wanted to kiss you last night."

"Why didn't you?" The question had formed and presented itself before she'd thought better of it.

Wyatt wet his lips, unmoving, unspeaking.

Violet waited, her gaze locked on his. The fear of rejection cresting anew.

He dropped his attention to her mouth, sending her insides into a spin.

"Wyatt," she whispered. "Say something."

He lifted a suddenly heated gaze to her eyes. "I was being a gentleman."

"And now?"

Wyatt slid a steady hand against her jaw, long fingers caressing her cheek, his broad thumb brushing over her bottom lip. "Now I'm just a man." He lowered his mouth to hers slowly, purposefully, never releasing her from that steady gaze.

The electricity she'd felt at his side or standing toe-to-toe on the porch was nothing compared to the power that coursed through her when his mouth moved against hers. Caressing, searching, giving. Her limbs were soft with pleasure, and longing circled in her core. It was the kind of kiss Violet had always wanted, but had never before experienced. The kind that made women half crazy with desire until they believed anything was possible.

Even a real, true, toe-curling, ballad-worthy love.

Chapter Fourteen

Violet hated to leave the lake behind. Things felt different there, more hopeful and less tragic. Take that cheek-pinkening, heart-pounding kiss for example. That was the power of the lake. Unfortunately, that sweet moment couldn't last. A clock was ticking back in their reality, and finding whatever Mary Alice had been looking for was top priority.

Wyatt matched Violet's pace on the way back to the house. She tried not to stare at his conflicted face or ask him about his thoughts. It had been her experience that the person asking often didn't like the answer, and Wyatt hadn't spoken since breaking off their kiss. He'd looked at her for a long moment with mind-melting intensity, then suggested they should get going. Not exactly what she'd been thinking at the moment, but she supposed it was nice of him to take her mind off things for a while.

He delivered Grandma's quilt to the back porch, then opened the door for her to pass.

Violet offered Sawyer a smile, then went straight upstairs for a shower. A cold one.

She managed to re-dress and blow-dry her hair into soft, cascading waves before Maggie woke from her nap. Violet told herself the extra swipes of mascara and lip gloss had nothing to do with the big brown-eyed man in her kitchen. She checked her finished reflection in the mirror and did her best not to recall the feeling of Wyatt's skilled lips on hers. She doubted her mouth would ever be the same. Or her heart, for that matter.

Maggie made a soft noise, drawing Violet's attention to the crib where her baby simply rolled over and continued to sleep peacefully.

Violet left the bedroom door open on her way out. She tugged the hem of her black cutoffs and adjusted the neckline of her baby blue satin tank top on her way back to the kitchen.

The men looked up when she arrived.

Wyatt's jaw sank open.

Sawyer gave an appreciative nod. "Welcome back."

"Thanks," Violet said, pleased with the responses, especially Wyatt's. "How's it going?"

Wyatt worked his mouth shut and clapped a hand on Sawyer's shoulder. "We split the list of wells into groups by location. Sawyer's going to take the farthest set first, then work his way back toward town. You, Maggie and I will drive past some of the closer locations and see if any are visible from the road. I've got a feeling the wells most easily accessible have been completely decommissioned by now, but it's worth a look. I figured we can help eliminate some possibilities before we go to the hospital."

"Hospital?" Violet asked. "I want to see Grandma,

but you must have plenty of research to do while Sawyer is well-hunting. I don't want to slow you down." How much time did she have left now? Could she even be sure the one who'd written the note would truly wait two days before doing whatever awful thing he had planned next?

"We can do both," Wyatt said. "I'll make time."

Sawyer stood and arched his back in a deep stretch, showcasing an undeniably fit physique. His lids drooped over crystal-blue eyes as he straightened. He was probably devastatingly handsome beneath the shaggy hair and beard, but Violet suspected he hid just as much behind the cocky grin and aloof facade as the disheveled-chic look he was rocking. She'd thought of asking Wyatt about Sawyer's story more than once, but she'd kept the question to herself, certain Wyatt would take his friend's secrets to the grave, whatever they were.

"I'm taking the truck today," Sawyer said. "If someone gets hauled off to jail again, it might as well be me."

Wyatt smiled. "Might as well."

Thirty minutes later, they were all on their way out.

Wyatt locked the front door behind them as their little tribe dispersed. Sawyer on his way to investigate abandoned wells. Wyatt, Maggie and Violet to perform a little drive-by reconnaissance on their way to the hospital.

She watched thick green foliage blur past her window and a pair of small white clouds sail across a perfect blue sky. If only her thoughts were half as clear as that sky. "What if the sheriff finds Sawyer on private property and does something irrational?" she asked. A few gruesome possibilities jolted into her mind. "At least you had me as a witness when he went bonkers before."

"Sawyer's fine. Sawyer is vapor," Wyatt said. "No one sees him unless he wants them to." His jaw set and he cast Violet a dark look before sticking his attention back to the road. "The sheriff won't find Sawyer."

"But what if he does? What if he tries to hurt him? There's no one around to stop him from doing anything crazy."

Wyatt slid mischievous eyes in Violet's direction. "In that highly unlikely scenario, I'd be more worried about the sheriff's safety than Sawyer's."

Violet felt her brows rising over her forehead. "You're saying Sawyer's dangerous?" A memory swept to the forefront of her mind. Hadn't Sawyer told her as much the night they'd met? *I'm not dangerous to you, but I definitely am dangerous.*

"I'm saying he's been through a lot, and a cocky small-town sheriff isn't going to get the best of him."

Violet considered his words. Sawyer had also said he was newly discharged. She didn't know how long he'd been enlisted, but it didn't take a professional to see that he'd been through some things. "Is he okay?"

"No," Wyatt answered flatly. "Sawyer's highly trained and severely post-traumatic, so I'm hoping for everyone's sake that no one around here ticks him off."

A chill slid down Violet's spine as she let that sink in.

Wyatt slowed at the next crossroads. A giant wooden sign stood reverently near the corner.

Violet focused her attention on the cracked and peeling white paint instead of whether or not she'd been reckless to leave Maggie alone with Sawyer earlier.

A series of black block letters splayed across the chipping paint, spelling the words *Potter's Field*.

Wyatt crawled to a stop beside the sign. "Did the librarian say she met Mary Alice at Potter's Field?"

"Yeah, and according to my grandpa, it used to be a hangout for vagrants and hippies," she said with a chuckle. "He loved to tell stories about the whole place being covered in tents and young travelers making love, not war."

Wyatt wheeled the Jeep in a new direction, traveling the length of the field. He watched Violet with a broad smile. "Wonder what the librarian was doing here."

Violet laughed. "Who knows? She was young then, too."

Wyatt rolled to another stop on the desolate country road. He peered across the cab and out Violet's window at the lush green land. "This might've been a wild hangout fifty years ago, but all I'm seeing today is soybeans."

"Times change, I guess," Violet said. "Maybe we'll have better luck looking for the wells." Her phone rang and she turned the screen to face her. "It's Tanya," she said, the familiar bud of panic pushing through her too-temporary calm. "Hello?"

"Hey," her cousin's voice was pert and chipper.

Violet sighed in relief. Not bad news then. "Hey," she said. "What's new?"

"Well, the doctor has given us the green light to

move Grandma. He says she's stable, and her vitals are strong, so there's no reason to keep her here if you'd prefer to move her to another facility. There are four within an hour's drive from here. You could stay at her place and make the commute if you wanted, at least until school started. That way, we'd both have easy access to her, and I'm sure she'll wake any day now, so we don't even have to think long-term like that."

Violet stilled. She didn't want to upset her cousin, but Tanya seemed to be missing the point that Grandma was in danger. What was she thinking by suggesting they move her to a place nearby? "That's great news, but I think we need to get her farther away from here than an hour's drive, and I definitely can't stay at her place. It's not safe, and I need to get back to Winchester."

Silence gonged through the phone.

Violet looked to Wyatt, who gave a stiff dip of his chin and orchestrated a three-point turn on the empty road, directing the Jeep toward the hospital.

Violet mouthed the words *thank you*. Sometimes it was as if Wyatt could read her mind. It was helpful at the moment, and utterly humiliating when he caught her daydreaming. About him.

"We'll be there soon," Violet said. She could hear Tanya breathing softly through the line, though she hadn't spoken in several long seconds. "I don't want to take Grandma away from you. I know your schedule will make it hard to see her, but we need to keep her safe until this is over." Violet's heart pinched. The ever-ticking clock said that wouldn't be long now. One way or another.

"I know," Tanya said. "I just wish she'd wake up."

"Me, too."

The CB radio on Sawyer's dashboard crackled. A fuzzy male voice rattled out a list of acronyms, then directed an ambulance and available unit to a too-familiar address.

Wyatt jammed the gas pedal, fishtailing over the asphalt.

"That's Grandma's address," Violet said, stunned.

Something bad was happening there. Again.

Violet gritted her teeth against a load of horrendous thoughts and possibilities. "Tanya," she said. "I've got to go."

Wyatt parked Sawyer's Jeep on the gravel lane outside Grandma's house and jumped out. He hauled Maggie onto one hip before shutting the doors.

Violet met them at the front bumper. She passed Wyatt's phone back to him. "Grandma's in the hospital. We're here, and Sawyer's in the field. So who needs an ambulance?"

She'd sent a series of text messages to Sawyer via Wyatt's phone, confirming his safety and whereabouts while Wyatt piloted the Jeep. Sawyer sent a selfie of himself on a rope in rappelling gear and wearing a miner's hat. She'd presumed he was inside a well, but he didn't add a caption to the photo, and she didn't ask. Wherever he was, it wasn't Violet's grandma's place.

An EMT jogged in their direction as they moved up

the rutted drive on foot. He stopped outside the closed doors of an ambulance.

"Excuse me," Wyatt called. "This is my girlfriend's grandma's house. We're staying here while Mrs. Ames is in the hospital, but it's just us." He lifted his gaze to a pair of EMTs guiding a gurney toward the barn. "So what's going on?"

Violet curled a warm hand around his elbow and leaned against his side.

The young man pulled the ambulance's back doors wide. "We received a call about an elderly white female…"

His answer was cut off by the approach of a blaring siren and sound of skidding tires on gravel.

"What the hell is this?" Sheriff Masterson yelled, stomping his way up the drive from the newly arriving vehicle. The lights on top of his cruiser continued to spin behind him.

The EMT paled. "I'm sorry, sir, but she appears to have fallen from the hay loft."

"Who?" Violet asked. "You haven't told us anything, and it's starting to scare me."

Wyatt didn't need to wait for an answer. He'd heard him clearly before, *an elderly white female*. There was only one person that could be.

A pair of men in matching EMT uniforms hustled toward the open ambulance bay with a loaded gurney.

Mary Alice Masterson was strapped aboard.

Mr. Masterson followed them, hands shoved deep in his pockets, gaze fixed to the ground.

The sheriff's hard eyes went round. "Mama?" He

shoved his way to the woman's side and gripped her hand in his. "She's going to be okay," he said, shooting an icy look at each EMT.

The grayest of the EMTs forced a tight smile. "The sooner we get her to the hospital, the more we'll know more about her injuries."

Sheriff Masterson fell back a step. Tears formed in his eyes as he stroked her gray hair. "Okay." He accepted the answer and allowed the men room to load his mother into the bay.

"Would you like to ride with her?" an EMT asked.

It was unclear if he'd meant to address Mary Alice's husband or son. They stood side by side now, glaring at each other.

"No, thank you," the sheriff ground the words out. "I'll take the cruiser, and Dad can ride with me."

Violet turned to Mr. Masterson. "What was she doing back in the barn?" Her voice was low and careful, but she held him in her stare. "You just took her away from here."

His jaw clenched and released, but he didn't speak.

Violet nearly vibrated with frustration at Wyatt's side. She turned her gaze on the sheriff. "No one's been in that barn for years, and now your mother was the second woman to fall from the hayloft this week. Don't you think that's a strange coincidence?"

Sheriff Masterson narrowed his eyes.

Wyatt pulled her against him. "I think we'd better go inside." The Masterson men looked as if they were close to a brawl, and Wyatt didn't want any part of their family feud. Not with Violet and Maggie so close by.

She dug her heels in briefly, but allowed him to walk her to the front door.

They watched from the window as the father and son climbed into the sheriff's cruiser and drove away.

Violet dropped the curtain and reached for her baby, who went to her with a smile. "I think that man just shoved his sick wife out of Grandma's hayloft, then called an ambulance to pretend it was an accident."

The same thought had crossed Wyatt's mind. And something more. "It might not have been an accident she wound up there this morning, either."

"You don't think she slipped away like he said," Violet guessed, passing Maggie to Wyatt. "You think he let her come here earlier so that when he did this we would all say, 'Oh, yeah, she was just up there ranting earlier.'"

"Maybe," he said, "or we could've interrupted his plan the first time."

The former sheriff was a fox in old man's clothing if Wyatt had ever seen one. He was sure of it. Problem was, his son wasn't going to dig into this. If his mom died, he'd go down in local history as the guy who arrested his dad for murdering his sick mom. The great Masterson legacy of Grove County would be ruined.

"That's really disturbing," Violet said. "You know what else I think?" Her face lit as she brushed past him on her way to the home's rear. "I think Mary Alice is the most honest Masterson we've met, and she believes a box of Henry Davis's things is in that barn. Maybe we just haven't looked in the right place yet."

Chapter Fifteen

Wyatt joined Violet in the barn, curiosity winding through him. Was she right? Had they simply missed something each time they'd been out here?

She took Maggie from his arms and began rocking her hips the moment her baby was nestled against her. "If I had something important to hide, I'd put it someplace no one would look. This seems like the perfect place, and Mary Alice obviously agrees." Violet's hand was protective on Maggie's head as she moved, holding her baby close.

"Can't hurt to give it another look," Wyatt said, watching the Ames ladies drift through filtered sunlight in the dusty old space.

"Let's split up," Violet said. "I'll start on that end. You start here."

Wyatt smiled as she walked briskly away. He'd spent years commanding troops of battle-weary men, but lately he was the one taking orders. Mostly from a brown-haired beauty and her baby.

He couldn't help recalling the news that Mary Alice had let slip that day on her porch. Violet's mom had run off and left her. Maggie would certainly never have to worry about that or wonder if she was loved. That fact was written all over her mother's face and etched into everything she did. A useless thread of anger curled in him when he thought of anyone who'd willingly leave their child behind. Another reason he was glad he didn't know Maggie's father.

Violet moved slowly along the far wall, dragging her fingers over the aged wood. Sunlight blazed through a second-story window, backlighting her silhouette and emphasizing the tantalizing shape beneath her sexy tank top. At her height, and in those shorts, her trim, tanned legs seemed to go on forever, and his gaze traveled the length of them to the hem of her cutoffs, then the images arrived unbidden. Her legs across his lap. Her legs around his hips.

Wyatt swallowed a groan and forced his head to turn away. Never had a woman so easily derailed his focus. If the Mastersons weren't eventually the death of him, he had a sneaking suspicion Violet Ames soon would be.

He traced a path along the barn's perimeter, taking his time but seeing nothing he hadn't on his previous trips inside.

Violet's soft voice carried on the air as she sang to Maggie.

Wyatt dared another look in their direction, and his heart tightened. He admired her dedication to her daughter and her grandma. It was clear that family meant everything to her, and that meant everything to Wyatt. The idea of having Violet and Maggie in his life permanently rushed over him like a freight train. It was a dogged and unrelenting notion these days. *What if she wants that, too?* The kiss she'd leveled him with by the lake hadn't helped. The more time he spent with her, the more time he wanted.

Unfortunately, it didn't matter that Wyatt's family and friends would love Violet and Maggie, or that they would be safe, adored and happy with him. Right now, all that mattered was that he finish the job he'd started with as much integrity as possible. He needed to keep his carpooling, pancake-burning fatherhood fantasies out of it. Violet needed a professional security agent to protect her. So that was what she would get.

"Wyatt?" Violet called.

He moved immediately toward the beacon tugging at his core. "Yeah?"

"Look." She crouched on the floor beside Maggie, who had already begun to crawl to him.

Wyatt scooped her up and kept moving. "What do you have there?"

"I'm not sure." Violet slid her fingertips along the floorboards with sheer concentration on her brow. "There's a knothole here, but the more I look at it, the more it seems man-made. There was a big wooden storage unit here when I was young. I suppose the hole could've been caused by moving that."

Wyatt worked the phone from his pocket and turned his flashlight app on the boards, where Violet worked diligently to get a fingerhold.

The light scattered, reaching deep beneath the wood.

He tented his brows is disbelief. "There's a room down there."

Violet rolled back on her haunches. "You're kidding. I was only hoping for a small compartment with the mystery box inside. Is it a root cellar? Tornado shelter?"

"Let's see." Wyatt set Maggie aside with a kiss, then passed his phone to Violet. "You work the light, and I'll see if I can get in there somehow."

Together, they found the hinges, camouflaged within the floorboards. The trapdoor rumbled open with a long, lamenting groan.

A puff of pride filled Wyatt's chest at the shock on Violet's face. "You've got a good eye. I'm not sure I'd have noticed this if I walked over it a dozen times."

She pulled Maggie onto her lap. "Thanks."

He gauged the small drop, then braced his hands on either side of the opening. "No problem. Now, keep that light going."

"Wait! You aren't going down there, are you?"

Wyatt jumped into the hole. "Yep." He lifted his arm overhead. "Not deep." He reached a hand up through the hole. "Mostly dirt."

"See anything?"

"Nah. Can you shine the light around me?"

Violet tapped his phone against his head. "You're too big. You're blocking everything."

Wyatt took the phone and shuffled around the cramped space, using the narrow beam as his guide. He checked the floor, walls and boards overhead until a yellowed cigar box appeared, tightly wedged in a nook above him. Without the light he would have only seen an empty cellar. Would've walked right by it just like the carefully carved knothole in the floor.

Wyatt set the box on the barn floor near Violet and Maggie. He hoisted himself back out of the little room and secured the trapdoor behind him. "You want to do the honors?"

Violet caught him in her warm gaze. "No."

Wyatt smiled. He flipped the box's lid open, exposing a set of someone's personal belongings: an antique watch, dog tags from the 1960s and a worn leather wallet.

"Henry Davis?" Violet asked.

Wyatt turned the box around for a better look at the metal tags. "Yeah." He shifted onto one hip and pulled a handkerchief from the back pocket of his jeans. He didn't want to disturb the missing man's things, but he had to know if the wallet was his, as well. He used the thin cloth to open the bifold. A Kentucky driver's license confirmed the owner of that item, as well. "Henry Davis."

Violet released a shaky sigh.

Wyatt helped her to her feet, box tucked carefully beneath his arm.

"I was hoping the box contained some old love letters," she said, dusting off her baby and her backside. "Something personal that Mary Alice didn't want her husband to see. This is much more unnerving."

She was right. A man didn't just leave his wallet and dog tags behind. Unless he left in a hurry or didn't want to be found.

"What do you think this means?" she asked.

"Nothing good." Wyatt led the way back to the house and locked them inside when they got there. "I need to let Sawyer know about this. He might want to change his search based on our find."

Violet set Maggie in her high chair and offered her a shaker of Cheerios. "In what way?"

"Well—" Wyatt dialed Sawyer's cell "—when he left, he was looking for anything out of the ordinary. Nothing specific. Maybe a box." He mimed the cigar box's size with his palms.

"And now?"

Wyatt pressed the phone to his ear. The icy slick of instinct sliding like a shiv into his gut. "Now I think we're looking for Henry Davis."

VIOLET TRIED NOT to panic as Wyatt drove Sawyer's Jeep off the road and onto the unplowed area alongside Potter's Field. Sawyer had insisted they come out and meet him when Wyatt called to tell him about the cigar box. He hadn't said why, but she had a solid guess that whatever it was wouldn't be good.

Wyatt parked the Jeep beside his truck in a clearing of dirt and gravel, then waved to Sawyer in the distance.

Violet climbed down, heart hammering, throat thick.

She freed Maggie from her car seat and slipped her into the baby sling positioned across her hip and adjusted a white eyelet bonnet over Maggie's soft brown curls, tilting the brim until Maggie no longer squinted against the sun.

Coming out here to see what had Sawyer so wound up hadn't been Violet's first choice, but staying home alone was so far at the bottom of her list she couldn't see it. So she'd decided to suck it up and go for the drive.

"Took you long enough," Sawyer yelled, closing the space between them. "I hope you brought me some water."

Wyatt tossed him the bottle he'd brought along from Grandma's fridge, then waited as Violet made her way to their sides. "Okay. Gang's all here. What did you find?"

Violet braced herself for the answer. *Not Henry Davis's remains. Not Henry Davis's remains*, she chanted internally.

"See for yourself." Sawyer turned and marched around the back side of a row of stately evergreen trees. "For starters, these pines are about fifty years old," he said.

Violet wrinkled her nose. She nearly laughed out loud. "And?"

"And I figure they were planted to hide this." He ducked under a line of barbed wire and walked to the edge of a circle made of bricks and covered in plywood. "Every other well I've visited today has either been decommissioned by the state, or is covered in rotted, dilapidated, ancient plywood. Every other well has been long forgotten."

Wyatt lifted the wire for Violet to duck beneath. "This is also covered in plywood."

"Correct." Sawyer's crystal eyes twinkled. "But this

is covered in nice, well-maintained plywood, and it's also the only abandoned well in the county that sits on a property owned by Old Man Masterson." He nodded slowly as Wyatt cocked his head. "Now ask me when he bought this lovely landlocked parcel."

"Fifty years ago?" Violet guessed.

"Round about," Sawyer answered. "This property is landlocked. It's no good for home building and it's junk for hunting, so why buy it at all? Why plant those trees in front of this well? And why is this the only well that hasn't been decommissioned by the state? Why is it covered in good, solid plywood?"

Violet stepped through the fallen and crunchy pine needles on the ground, nausea ripping at her insides.

Wyatt circled the well, then took one large step away and circled again, tracking his gaze across the ground. Searching.

Sawyer hiked a foot onto the new plywood and cast his attention around them, taking in the larger picture. "We're at the edge of the property, but a barbed wire fence is set up about thirty feet out, making its own perimeter with the well at the center. No-trespassing signs are nailed to the corner posts."

Violet gave the now-distant Potter's Field a long look. "Maybe the previous sheriff bought this property to stop all the wild parties. My grandpa ranted about what a nuisance the folks were in Potter's Field and about all the litter they left behind."

Sawyer gave the adjacent field a curious look. "I think the sheriff could have kept folks off that land without buying the property next door. Besides, no one has ever lived here. They can't. No road frontage. This would only be good for farming, and no one's farming it." He nodded toward the neighboring soybean rows. "They're farming right up to it, then that's it."

Wyatt ducked into a squat about ten feet from the well and gave a worrisome whistle. "Sawyer?"

Sawyer's head jerked in Wyatt's direction. His frame went on alert. "Yes, sir." He jogged to his friend's side.

Something in Wyatt's voice had the same effect on Violet. Her limbs were wooden. Her feet heavy. Wyatt had found something, and she was certain it wasn't anything good.

"What is it?" Violet's heart took off at a runner's pace.

Wyatt extended his palm at her like a crossing guard. "Wait."

He looked up as Sawyer approached. "This looks like an old land mine. That can't be right, can it? Surely no one would…"

The distinctive *click* beneath Violet's shoe stopped his sentence along with her heart. Whatever her foot had landed on, it didn't belong in an empty field. It wasn't more pine needles. Not a fallen branch. Or a pine cone or debris.

"Don't move," Wyatt warned, his handsome face pale with shock and fear. He straightened slowly, carefully, as if he were the one about to take his last breath instead of her.

She could see it written in his stance, his sad, almost sickened gaze. Violet had also found a land mine.

"No!" Maggie said, clapping her hands at the sight of Wyatt headed her way.

Tears pooled in Violet's eyes, stinging her nose and blurring her vision. "Wyatt," she sobbed. How could she have been so careless?

"Shh," he cooed, examining her feet as he crept closer.

Both men approached with caution. Knees slightly bent, arms forward, eyes wide. They came at her in a vee, moving in from opposite angles, as if they were cornering a wild animal.

"Be very still," Sawyer said. "Don't move your feet." He dropped into a crouch before her and moved the parched grass.

A choked warble escaped her tightening throat.

"No!" Maggie jerked forward again, nearly throwing herself from the baby sling, nearly forcing Violet's weight to shift fatally on the aged mine plate. "No!" she sang, chubby fists opening and closing, wanting Wyatt as he neared.

Despair clawed through Violet's chest. She saw the truth in Wyatt's eyes. There was no saving her, but she wouldn't accept this fate for Maggie. Her heart rent in two at the possibility that this was the end for her daughter. It couldn't be. Not now. Not like this. Not Maggie.

"Wyatt," Violet cried. "Save my baby."

Chapter Sixteen

Wyatt couldn't respond. His mind worked overtime, scrutinizing the situation, recalling the other mine he'd just seen. Considering its age. Potential instability. And the possibility it would go off simply because Violet had stepped on it, instead of waiting for the pressure to release.

Sawyer inched past him. He took Maggie into his arms, then dipped his chin at Violet. His cool blue eyes locked on Wyatt. "I'll get her away from here. Try not to be too stupid."

Wyatt flickered a look in his friend's direction. "Stupid is a matter of opinion."

"Wyatt." Violet's voice was a desperate quivering mess. "Go with her. Stay with her."

"Give me a minute," he said slowly. His mind raced through probabilities and calculations. With Sawyer and Maggie out of the way, he had an idea that might not kill them both. It wasn't a great one, but they were out of time for those.

"Please," Violet pushed. "Take care of Maggie. I can stand here until I know you're long gone. She doesn't have to see, and she won't remember. It's okay. Just, please, go. Protect her."

The pain and sacrifice of her words seared through him. "Remain calm," he said, inching away.

"She's going to be orphaned. Just like me. But I'm okay because I was loved. Tanya will take her. Tanya will love her."

Wyatt paced away, his hardened heart reduced to mush. "Do not shift your weight off that plate."

"I won't," Violet vowed. "Make sure my baby knows I loved her more than I've ever loved anyone or anything. More than she can possibly imagine." Tears rushed down her cheeks, dripping over her lips and falling freely from her chin and jaw.

The Jeep's engine revved to life. "Hey, Stone," Sawyer called through the open window, his voice clearly carrying over the long distance. "What's the plan?"

"Take care of my baby!" Violet screamed, hot eyes flashing at Sawyer. "Get out of here!"

Wyatt raised his hand to Sawyer. "Back up about a hundred yards." He turned to Violet. "Do you trust me?"

"What?" She wiped her tears and watched him with keen curiosity. "What are you doing? Why did you stop? Why aren't you leaving?"

Wyatt backed up another three steps. "Do you trust me?" he repeated.

"Yes."

He lowered into a sprinter's stance. "Then don't fight the impact," he said. "Just let it happen."

Violet's chin swung left, then right. "No. Get out of here! Protect Maggie!"

"One," Wyatt said.

"No! You'll be killed!"

"Two."

"Wyatt!"

He launched forward on angry, determined legs, propelling himself through the grass at top speed, barreling toward the woman he loved. He would not let her die. Would not let her sweet baby become an orphan. Not now. Not ever. And not on his watch.

He lowered his frame to reduce his center of gravity on impact, planting his hard shoulder into her soft middle and tossing her easily with him through the air. Their bodies collided with the smack and crunch of flesh and bone.

The explosion that followed was teeth-rattling. Wyatt's ears rang, and dirt and debris rained over them in hunks and patches. Sticks, rocks and chunks of earth pelted them as they bounced against the hard ground and rolled to a stop at the barrier of pine trees.

Violet's scream was silenced upon impact.

Wyatt's vision blurred as he struggled to pull his lids open and set the world straight once more. Images of battlefields from his past mixed frighteningly with the one thing that mattered in his present. Violet. He pulled himself into the moment, forcing memories away and his body onto bruised and bloodied forearms. "Violet." His voice was foreign to his ears, too low and gravelly. The blurry image of her swayed before him. His head pounded and ached. His heart took a deep cutting blow when she didn't answer. "Wake up," he ordered, but her arms lay limply at her sides, face rolled slightly away, eyes closed. She was motionless save for the shallow rise and fall of her chest and a blessedly still-beating heart.

Wyatt scrambled to her, forcing his vision to clear and reaching for her sweet face.

A thick smear of crimson covered her exposed cheek and ear. The unmistakable shape of a flat gray stone was visible beneath her head, scattered over with pine needles and long brown hair. "No." He forced himself onto his knees. "Violet," he demanded. "Violet!" He'd taken the brunt of the blast with his back as they flew. She should have been okay. Wyatt searched her throat for the heartbeat he needed to feel, slow but strong.

"Wyatt?" Sawyer's voice registered nearby. He appeared then, darting through the trees to Wyatt's side. Maggie cried on his hip, arms reaching for her mother, but Violet didn't stir. "Do you want an ambulance out here?" Sawyer asked.

"No." Wyatt curled a motionless Violet into his arms and pushed himself onto aching legs. "I don't want the son of a bitch responsible for those mines to know we found his hiding spot. You protect Maggie. I'll get Violet to the ER, then we'll come back here tonight, find out what's hidden in that well." Wyatt's long purposeful strides ate up the distance as they tracked through the woods, back to their vehicles, away from the well and the booby traps around it. "We're going to need help from outside this godforsaken town if we want justice served."

"You want me to hunt down that deputy?" Sawyer asked. "Santos?"

"No. Take Maggie home and guard her with your life," Wyatt instructed. "I'll be there as soon as I can. Then we'll figure this out together."

"Yes, sir."

The drive to the hospital was excruciating. Every dip in the road and jostle of his frame hurt bone deep. Worse than that, his constant prayer for Violet's eyes to open wasn't answered.

He left his truck outside the emergency room entrance, doors open, engine running.

"We need help," he called as the glass doors parted. Violet's motionless body lay over his arms. Blood from her head clung to his shirt and skin. "Help us!" he demanded, using the full power of his deep tenor to command attention.

A man in a white coat turned his way, followed by a pair of nurses. The trio snapped into action, rushing to his side.

"What happened?" the doctor asked.

"I'm not sure," Wyatt lied. He hadn't taken time to think of a proper story on the drive over, and he didn't want to tell them about the land mine. He and Violet had escaped the worst of the explosion. Their injuries were mostly a result of their graceless landing. Besides, once the sheriff knew they'd been so close to his well, Wyatt was sure whatever had been hidden there for fifty years would be moved immediately. "We hit our heads when we fell," he finally said. "She landed on a rock. She's bleeding."

The doctor pulled Violet's eyelids open and shone a light into them while the nurses ran for a gurney. Together, the team strapped Violet down and wheeled her to a station stocked with supplies. A nurse started an IV drip. The doctor checked her vitals. They administered triage to her cuts, scrapes and bruises. The questions came rapid-fire as they worked. "How long has she been unconscious? How far did you fall? Where were you when it happened?"

Wyatt claimed that they had been hiking, enjoying the view from a significant height when the trail gave way along the edge. They fell a great distance, tumbling over rocks, limbs and roots.

Soon, Wyatt was pushed back and a curtain was pulled around them as they worked.

Wyatt collapsed onto an empty chair against the wall. He bent forward at the waist, catching his face in open palms and doing his best to hold himself together.

The sounds and scents of the hospital crept into his scrambled thoughts, taking him back overseas. Flashing memories of other terrifying times. Other injured loved ones. He pressed his fingers hard against his temples, forcing images of war from his mind.

"Looks like a slight concussion." The doctor's voice was back. Close again.

Wyatt jerked onto his feet, blinking away the past and pulling the moment at hand back to light. "Will she be okay?"

The doctor hugged a clipboard to his chest. "Sure. She's suffered extensive lacerations and contusions, but they'll heal. The bruised ribs will take time." He grimaced. "It's as if she hit a tree on her way down. We put something in her IV for the pain and stitched her head."

"Thank you." One hot tear blazed a trail over Wyatt's icy cheek. He took the doctor's hand in his and shook it hard. "Thank you."

The doctor kept hold of his hand. "She said not to let you leave without an exam."

"She's awake?" He dragged the doctor toward the curtain.

The doctor caught Wyatt's elbow in his free hand. "Not until I take a look at you."

Wyatt kept moving. He had nearly a foot and probably fifty pounds on the little man beside him. "I want to see her." He ducked through the barrier and felt a mound of tension roll away.

"Hey," she said softly. Her head was wrapped in white gauze. Her arms were spattered with bandages and dark with bruises.

"Violet." He stroked hair from her cheeks. "I'm so sorry."

She batted glossy eyes. "You saved our lives."

Wyatt lifted her small hand to his face and a hot streak swiveled over his cheekbone.

"Hey." Violet wiped the single tear away. "We're okay," she whispered. "Because of you."

Wyatt leaned over the silver bed rail, gathering her in his arms and burying his face in her soft brown hair. It wasn't the right time to tell her that he loved her, but he'd never been so sure of anything in his life, and he would tell her one day soon. What she did with the information was up to her. Nothing would diminish that truth.

Violet peeked over his shoulder, sweeping her gaze through the room. "Where's Maggie? I want to see her. Is Sawyer in the waiting room?"

"No. They aren't here, but they're safe. He won't let anyone hurt her."

The doctor cleared his throat. "I'd better have a look at you."

Wyatt spun around. He'd nearly forgotten they weren't alone. "Go for it." He squeezed Violet's hand, unwilling to let her go. There was so much he wanted to say, but the timing was awful, and the emotions were raw and new. He wasn't sure where to start. He could see a future with Violet and Maggie. The kind his folks had with him. The kind he'd given up on when he joined the service. A near decade of army life had changed him. Hardened him. But Violet and Maggie were changing him back. Excavating the man he'd started out to be.

Her hand curled over his wrist as the doctor moved into view, flashing his penlight into Wyatt's eyes. "Will you check on Grandma when the exam is finished?" Violet asked. "Maybe ask Tanya to come down here if she's on duty? I need to get those transfer papers filled out." She lifted an apologetic face to him as the doctor stepped away. "Maggie and I can't stay. It's just too dangerous to be here any longer than is absolutely necessary."

Wyatt pressed a kiss to her forehead, inhaling the

sweet scent of her and making a memory he hoped would last. "It's okay."

He gave the doctor another two minutes to finish his job before shaking him off. "Thanks," he said then, interrupting the instructions he'd heard a dozen times before. "Aspirin. Ice. Rest. Water. Got it."

Wyatt rode the elevator to the second floor in search of Violet's cousin Tanya and a quick visit with her grandma. He focused on his marching orders instead of the fact that accomplishing these tasks meant saying goodbye to Violet and Maggie.

A man in a hospital security uniform leaned his elbows on the nurse's desk, flirting with a young blonde. The chair outside Violet's grandma's room was empty.

"Hey," Wyatt complained. "Why aren't you watching room two fourteen?"

The man tented his brows at Wyatt, taking in his battered appearance. "She's fine. Old Sheriff Masterson's in there with her."

Wyatt swore. He hopped into a painful jog and rushed through the door to her room.

Mr. Masterson leaned over the comatose woman, his lips moving near her ear.

"What are you doing here?" Wyatt snapped. "Get away from her."

Mr. Masterson looked Wyatt over with a mischievous smile. "Well, what on earth has happened to you?"

Wyatt ground his teeth. "Get out."

Mr. Masterson crossed the room and stopped inside Wyatt's personal space. The old man was tall and broad. Bold and cocky. "You think I'm old," he said.

"You think I don't know what you've been up to, but this is my town, and I don't miss a thing."

Wyatt stood firm, squaring his shoulders and locking his jaw. "Stay away from this family."

"Believe me. I tried." He tossed a glance in Violet's grandma's direction. "Some people just won't listen."

"Knock knock." A smiling man in a gray suit, tie and glasses appeared in the door. "I hope I'm not interrupting anything. I'm Dr. Fisk. I've come to check on our Sleeping Beauty over there."

"I was just on my way out," Mr. Masterson said. "I've got lots to do today." He tipped his hat to the doctor, then left Wyatt with a withering smile.

Wyatt turned to face the frail-looking woman in the hospital bed. The clock was ticking, and he had to get her out of there before Masterson had a chance to finish what he'd undeniably started.

Chapter Seventeen

Violet sat on her grandma's living room floor, filling plastic totes with memories and praying they'd all get out of River Gorge alive. She wrapped a framed photo in newspaper, then set it on a stack of photo albums in another nearly full container. "I know I can't take everything, but it feels as if anything I leave is doomed for destruction."

Wyatt watched from the couch where he bounced Maggie on one knee. "Pack as much as you want. There's plenty of room in my pickup's bed, and I've got no problem renting a box truck if that's what you need."

"Thanks." Violet's head ached nearly as much as her body, but she'd never complain about anything as trivial as a headache again. Not after what she, Wyatt and Maggie had just been through. "The doctor said we can move Grandma tomorrow after breakfast. Whatever isn't packed by then can just stay. Meanwhile, this is a good distraction." Violet had nearly lost everything a few hours ago and the hollow feeling left behind in her gut felt like a warning. "I don't care what Grandma was looking into anymore. It's not worth dying over, and I just want to get her out of here before tomorrow night when my forty-eight hours are up."

Wyatt set Maggie on the floor, then lowered himself down beside her. "I'm sorry that you were ever in danger," he said, leveling her with sincere brown eyes. "None of that should have happened once I got here. I've failed miserably at that, but I won't leave without making sure whoever is behind these attempts on your life and your grandma's is arrested, even if it is the Mastersons."

Maggie patted Wyatt's jean-covered thigh and beamed up at him.

The look in his eyes was unfathomable, and Violet's heart twisted hard.

"What are you up to?" he asked Maggie.

Maggie leaned closer, grabbing tiny fistfuls of his cotton shirt, and pulled herself up to stand.

Violet's heart soared. "Oh my goodness."

Wyatt's eyes stretched wide. "Look at you!" He caught her under her arms and lifted her high into the air, weaving her over his head with a rumbling belly laugh before delivering her to Violet's hands.

She kissed her baby and hugged her tight. "Big girl," she sang. "You did it!"

"No!"

Wyatt snorted. He cupped the back of her head in one big hand and planted a kiss on her forehead. "Nice work, cowgirl."

Maggie clapped.

Violet's heart melted. She didn't want to separate them. Maggie had responded so profoundly to Wyatt's attention from the very start. She'd never seen anything like it, and it killed her to think this was the end. "You don't have to stay here, you know," she offered. "Grandma would understand, and she wouldn't want anyone to die over this."

Wyatt gave a tight smile. "I won't leave your side until you're settled in Winchester, but after that, I'm coming back to River Gorge to finish this. Your grandmother deserves that much, and so do you."

"It's not worth it," Violet said, firming up her tone. "Staying here is a bad idea. The Mastersons aren't right. We all need to leave. I'm not even sure Grandma will be safe in the new facility. I keep thinking of all the ways Sheriff Masterson could find out where we went and how easily he can get to us anywhere we go." She snuggled Maggie closer before returning her to the floor where she could practice her new trick again. "I don't know how to keep them safe, and it's terrifying." The awful note she'd found at the hospital had said as much. She couldn't keep everyone safe. She was only one person, and now she was injured and slow.

"You're right to leave," he said.

"Maybe. But you're here. Anywhere else I'll be on my own."

It was a conversation they'd had days ago, and the right answer wasn't any clearer now than it had been then.

Sawyer's Jeep growled up the drive to Grandma's house, country music rattling the windows before he killed the engine.

Wyatt rose to let him in.

Sawyer sauntered inside with a smile for Violet. "The guy at the body shop says your car will be finished in the morning. They've got the tires in stock, and they're planning to get them mounted and balanced when they reopen. I caught him on his way out for the night."

Deputy Santos climbed the porch steps and followed Sawyer inside.

Violet hadn't even heard a second vehicle over Sawyer's music. "Deputy Santos?"

Wyatt extended a hand to him, looking utterly unsurprised as always. "It was nice of you to come."

Sawyer clapped the deputy on his back. "He just wanted to make sure we're all doing okay after that near-death experience y'all had."

Deputy Santos cocked a brow. "What near-death experience? I'm here because you told me there had been another break-in."

Sawyer lifted his shoulders in an exaggerated shrug. "I lied. But you're already here, so you might as well come on in and hear about our day."

Wyatt locked the door behind them.

Violet pulled Maggie onto her hip, then led the men into the kitchen. Every step sent a current of pain and nausea through her. "Can I get you a cup of coffee?" she asked the deputy.

"No. Thank you." He looked to Sawyer, then Wyatt. "What's this about?" He scanned the room, stopping briefly on Wyatt's banged-up face before landing on Violet's bandaged head.

She touched the gauze nervously. "I have a slight

concussion," she said. "I was nearly blown up today." She slid Maggie into her high chair and posed her plastic pony on the tray.

Santos rubbed his stubble-covered cheeks and chin. "All right, I'm listening."

Wyatt deposited the cigar box of Henry Davis's things on the kitchen table. "We found this hidden in the floorboards of the barn out back."

Sawyer moved in closer. "The barn where all the old ladies keep taking suspicious spills." He passed the deputy a pair of latex gloves.

Santos opened the lid.

Violet poured herself some coffee, then began to talk. She explained everything they'd learned since last speaking to Deputy Santos. "So you see," she concluded, "if we're right about the sheriff and his father, we're going to need your help."

Santos swore. He ran a hand through thick black hair, then shut the box lid.

Sawyer produced a thumb drive from his pocket and offered it to their guest. "Everything you need to locate the well is on there. Several geographical and aerial maps and a copy of the deed to the land. Plus, all the notes Wyatt's made while visiting your lovely town."

Santos rolled his shoulders and rubbed his forehead. "I'll take a look. See what I come up with, but I've got to tell you, I've felt followed since that night I pulled you over. I'm pulling threads and being quiet, but it's slow work."

"We don't have time for slow, Deputy," Violet said. "I've got less than a day." She walked the deputy out, then watched as the cruiser's taillights disappeared into the night.

Sawyer lingered in the kitchen with Maggie.

Wyatt moved to stand behind her at the window. Heat from his skin burned through the soft fabric of her pajama top. She dared to lean back, and he accepted her weight easily, winding strong arms around her middle. "How are you doing?"

Their reflections stared back at her, and she loved what she saw there. Trust. Appreciation. Desire.

"Right now?" she said, finding a smile amid the pain. "Pretty good." Violet let herself have this moment. She wasn't ready to say goodbye to Wyatt, but he would soon be gone nonetheless. She rested her head against his chest, still admiring the view of their reflections.

"I won't leave your side until I know you're safe. I promise you that, but right now you should probably get some sleep. Big day tomorrow."

Violet turned in the small cocoon of his arms and clasped her hands behind his back. "What if I'm not ready to say goodbye to you?" she asked, feeling brave and arching against him for a better look at his face too high above hers.

Surprise flashed in his eyes, followed closely by pleasure. "Yeah?"

"Yeah."

He leaned forward, dropping his forehead against hers. "Then don't."

Sawyer arrived to wreck the moment, Maggie in his arms, pulling firmly on his ratty beard.

Violet rolled her head in his direction without letting Wyatt go.

"What?" Wyatt asked, tightening his hold on her.

"There's something else," Sawyer said.

Violet eased her grip on Wyatt. For a moment, she'd had hope. Grandma was being moved out of town tomorrow. A local, and hopefully honest, deputy was helping them look into things. Wyatt didn't want her to say goodbye.

And now Sawyer had arrived with bad news. She could feel it in her already achy bones.

"What?" Wyatt repeated, his voice deeper now.

"I got something on that demolition derby car you asked me to locate. I found one matching the description registered for the county fair about ten years back. An online article linked it to a man now in his eighties. I stopped at his place to ask about the car while I was out fetching Santos for you. Nice fellow. Confused though. He thought the car was in his outbuilding." Sawyer set Maggie on the floor and crossed his arms. "The man hadn't been out there to look at it in about eighteen months. He had a stroke, and he lives alone."

Violet considered the new information. "You think someone stole it. Anyone could've been behind the wheel."

Sawyer tipped his head side to side. "Possibly. Though Mary Alice Masterson frequently drove him to his medical appointments and did some shopping for him every week before she got sick. They knew each other when their kids were young."

Violet dropped her arms to her sides. "So Mr. Masterson probably knew about the car and that the car's owner would never miss it if he borrowed it. It's been him trying to get rid of me all along."

Wyatt rubbed a stubble-covered cheek. "You should've seen Masterson's face at the hospital. He knew when he saw me that I'd likely come head-to-head with one of his land mines, and he didn't even blink."

"Well," Sawyer said, "the good news here is that we've got nightfall working for us. He won't be able to get out there and mess with whatever's in the well until dawn."

Violet's adrenaline spiked as fear shot through her once more. "You aren't planning to go back out there tonight, are you?" Memories of her misstep and the telltale *click* of the land mine rushed to mind. She recalled perfectly the weight of Maggie in her arms. The terror on Wyatt's face. The all-encompassing pain that had taken hold of her as she'd struggled to find consciousness after the blast. "You can't."

Sawyer didn't answer.

"Tell him," she instructed Wyatt.

Violet's cell phone rang, instantly changing the direction of her panic. Tanya's number centered the screen. "Hello?"

"Violet?" Tanya asked, a tremor in her voice.

The urge to be sick nearly overtook her. Images of Mr. Masterson with a pillow pressed to her sleeping grandma's face or introducing something deadly to her IV pushed their way into mind. "Yes?"

"She's awake!" Tanya chirped. "Come on. She's asking for you. I have to do my rounds, but you should come!"

Violet was on her feet in a second, immediately swaying under the nausea and pain of her too-quick movement. "Grandma's awake."

Wyatt steadied her, then pulled Maggie into his arms. "I'll drive."

Sawyer walked them to the truck. "I'm going to gather my gear and see what's in that well."

Violet bobbed onto her toes and kissed his cheek. "Be careful," she said. "I doubt complaining will stop you, and I've got to go, so please, please watch yourself."

Sawyer turned a megawatt smile on Wyatt. "Your girl just kissed me."

Wyatt wrapped an arm around Violet's shoulders and shook his head. "Don't get any ideas."

"I can't keep the ladies away."

Violet let herself enjoy the flutter of butterflies in her chest as Wyatt easily accept Sawyer's accusation that she was his girl.

He opened the passenger door to his truck. "I figure all the bad guys recognize Sawyer's Jeep by now. That ruse is up. Might as well ride in style again."

She buckled in with a smile. Scents of earth and leather, cologne and spearmint clung to the cab's interior. Violet had to admit, she liked Wyatt's ride a whole lot better than Sawyer's.

Wyatt transferred Maggie's car seat from the Jeep, then tucked Maggie into it and snapped her five-point safety belt. He climbed behind the wheel and dragged his palm over the dash as if to welcome himself home. "Let's go meet Grandma."

VIOLET RAN AHEAD inside the hospital and called the elevator.

Wyatt trailed behind, seemingly in no hurry with Maggie in his arms, though his incredibly long strides delivered him easily to her side before the shiny doors were fully opened.

Violet fell back a step at the sight of the elevator car's passengers.

Sheriff Masterson and his father stepped out and rounded the corner away from them without speaking. The sheriff's face was red and knotted. His father's was a mask of disgust.

A woman in a gray pantsuit stepped on board ahead of Violet and Wyatt. Her name tag said Hospital Administrator. "Four, please."

Violet pressed the button, an idea forming in her mind. "The sheriff and his father were just here," she told the administrator. "They looked devastated. I hope Mary Alice hasn't taken another turn for the worse."

The woman gave Violet a curious look. "Are you friends of the family?"

"Yes," Violet improvised. "All my life, especially my grandmother and Mrs. Masterson."

"Oh." The administrator turned to Violet. The deep remorse of her disposition raised gooseflesh on Violet's arms. "I'm sorry to be the one to tell you, but I'm afraid Mary Alice is gone. She had an awful fall earlier, and in her current condition she just wasn't able to recover. Absolutely tragic. I'm very sorry for your loss. If there's anything I can do to help the family, you'll let me know?"

Violet wobbled her head in what she hoped resembled agreement. Then she slid her hand into Wyatt's. Mary Alice Masterson was gone. Would her grandma be next?

Wyatt squeezed her hand in reassurance, probably reading her thoughts as usual.

When the elevator opened on Grandma's floor, they darted out, hurrying hand in hand down the hall.

The empty chair outside her door sent the ugly images back to Violet's mind. Where was the hospital security she requested? Had the sheriff sent him away? If so, she could only imagine why and to what end. "Grandma!"

Violet skidded to a stop at the sight of her grandmother tilted up on her hospital bed. Wyatt slowed behind her.

A man in a hospital security uniform poured water from the pitcher on her bedside table. "Look at that, Mrs. Ames, you've been awake less than an hour and you already have company," he said, handing the cup to her. "I'll be right outside if you need me."

Grandma's eyes brimmed with tears that fell easily as she stretched her arms toward Violet. "Get over here."

Violet embraced her grandma, who kissed her cheeks a dozen times.

She touched the bandage on Violet's head with soft, careful fingers. "Oh, no." She slid teary eyes to the man standing at Violet's side. "Mr. Stone?"

Wyatt offered his hand. "Yes, ma'am. It's nice to finally meet you."

Emotion raced over her pale face and gathered on her brow. "You know what's happened, then?"

"No," Violet said. "Not really. We have guesses, but everything has been a real mess."

Her grandma examined Wyatt, taking him in head to toe. Her attention lingered on Maggie snuggled tightly against his broad chest. "Maggie?" she asked, with utter awe. She motioned Wyatt nearer and stroked Maggie's chubby legs when he reached the bed rails. She beamed at her great-granddaughter and tugged gently on her socked feet. "She's perfect."

"Thank you," Violet said with evident pride. "We're going to stay with you for as long as you need to heal, but right now I need to know what you know."

Grandma dragged her gaze from Maggie to Violet with a solemn nod. "It started when I had lunch on Mary Alice's porch last month," she said. Her brow furrowed. "How is she? Have you been over to see her while I've been out?"

Violet looked to Wyatt. She felt the words backing up in her throat.

"She's gone," he said, filling in the tragic blank. Regret clung to his handsome face. "I'm sorry. I know she meant a lot to you."

Grandma swallowed hard. "How did it happen?"

"She fell from your hayloft."

Grandma covered her mouth with one thin hand, then rested back against the bed. "Fell," she scoffed.

"Grandma," Violet pressed, hoping she wouldn't ask about Ruth next. Violet's heart couldn't take delivering more horrific news, and she wasn't sure Grandma was in any condition to accept more. Besides, they were all in danger, and that needed addressing immediately. "We really need to know what you know."

Grandma wiped the tears from her cheeks with trembling fingers. "Mary Alice spent our whole meal obsessing about a man she knew a long time ago. I only met him once, but Mary Alice was involved with him briefly before he went to war."

Wyatt shifted Maggie in his arms and patted her back gently when she began to wake. "Henry Davis?"

"That's right." She nodded slowly. "You found the box."

"Yes, ma'am," he said. "It's safe now."

"Good."

"Go on," Violet said, squeezing her grandma's hand.

"Mary Alice got involved with Tom after Henry was deployed. According to Mary Alice, he and Tom had words when Henry came to see her while he was on leave. That didn't surprise me. Tom was just a deputy then, but he was always a bully. Their son isn't much better." She looked from Violet to Wyatt. "Anyway, the rest of her story got gruesome from there. At first, I chalked it up to the dementia stealing her reality. Then I found just enough information online to make me wonder."

Violet's palms grew damp as she prepared for the

rest of the story. "Mr. Masterson killed Henry Davis, didn't he?"

Her grandmother sighed. "I think so. Mary Alice said Henry fell. Tom punched him, and he went down, but he hit his head on the well near Potter's Field and never got back up. She said Tom didn't want to go to jail over something that was an accident, so he tossed Henry's body in the well and neither of them spoke of it again. When she gave me that old cigar box, I knew I was in deep."

"I'm so sorry," Violet said.

"I didn't want to bring her story to authorities without basis, so I decided to try to back it up first. Then I'd contact someone outside the county sheriff's department for help."

"That's when you called Wyatt," Violet said.

"Yes." Grandma's composure cracked. She pulled a tissue from the box on her bedside stand.

"Reaching out for help was smart," Violet said. "Mr. Masterson is a mess. I think he's the reason you're in here, and now I'm certain you're lucky to be alive at all."

"Well," her grandma said, touching the bandage on her head, "seems like I wasn't as smart as I'd thought." She pressed a fresh tissue to the corner of one eye. "Mary Alice wanted that man's family to have his things and to know what really happened to him. She said they needed to know he wasn't a deserter, and she wanted him to have a proper military burial."

Wyatt cleared his throat. "I can see that he's interred properly."

"Thank you," Grandma whispered.

Violet pulled in a deep breath. Now they just needed to get Grandma in front of someone who could find justice for Henry Davis before anyone else wound up dead.

Chapter Eighteen

Wyatt's phone buzzed in his back pocket. He slid the device onto his palm and puzzled at the number on the screen. Local, but he didn't recognize it. "Wyatt Stone," he answered.

"This is Deputy Santos," the man said. "I think we need to talk."

Violet was on her feet, instinctively reaching for Maggie as if she could somehow sense the tension bunching in Wyatt's muscles.

Her grandma grabbed the bed's metal rail, straining closer. "What's wrong?"

Wyatt turned away, angling his torso for some privacy. "Where?" he asked Santos.

The deputy heaved a troubled sigh. "I don't know. There probably isn't an ideal location in this town."

"You found something?" Wyatt guessed. If the deputy believed them about the former sheriff, then they had an ally, and that was all they needed. That and maybe Henry Davis's remains. Wyatt wasn't sure Mrs. Ames's retelling of a dead woman's tale would be enough, especially considering Mary Alice's mental state at the time of the revelation.

"I took those things you gave me to a coffee shop at the end of my shift," Santos said, "and I gave them a long hard look. I had to admit the story was compelling, so I headed back to the department, thinking I'd slip onto my computer and look for more details in the cold cases. When I got there, my bottom drawer was unlocked. I never leave it unlocked. My files were askew. Key was in my pocket."

"Meet us back at the Ames house," Wyatt said. "Mrs. Ames woke from her coma tonight, and she filled in all those blanks we talked about."

"Yep." Santos disconnected.

Wyatt gave the trio of Ames ladies a long look. What was safest for them? All of them? "Violet, why don't you and Maggie stay here this time? You'll be safe. There's security at the door. Witnesses everywhere."

"No way." Violet stood with Maggie.

Wyatt lifted a palm. "I'll see what Santos found, then give you a call on my way back. I won't be long, and it will give you more time to visit with your grandma."

"No." She kissed her grandma's cheek. "I want to hear what Santos has to say. We can come right back after."

Grandma nodded. "Go. You're both safer guarded by him and all that military training than by me and my broken hip."

Tanya cruised into the room with a balloon and pink

plastic bag. "There you are." She hugged Violet, then tied the balloon string to the arm of the guest chair. "I clocked out early so I could run down to the gift shop and get you these before the shop closed." She upended the bag onto Grandma's legs. Magazines. *The Rose Parade. Garden Delight.* And *Country Lady.* Tanya's smile dimmed as she took in the faces around her. "What?"

"We have to run back to Grandma's place and check on something," Violet said. "Stay with Grandma?"

Tanya smiled. "Of course."

"I'll call if we learn anything significant," Violet said. "I'll try to come back tonight, but if Maggie falls asleep, I'll let her." She shifted her attention to her grandma, wishing for all the world that she could pull up a chair and stay with her every minute until she knew they were all safe. "Either way, I'll be back here first thing tomorrow to get you moved."

"Moved?" Grandma asked.

Tanya waved a hand. "I'll fill her in."

Violet nodded. "I'll see you soon, Grandma."

Wyatt took her hand and headed for the parking lot.

"THANK YOU," VIOLET SAID as the bright hospital lights faded into the night behind them.

Wyatt glanced her way, his profile strong and confident. "For what?"

"For letting me come along," she said. "For not fighting me on it. I know you want to protect me, and you wanted me to stay at the hospital."

Wyatt's sharp eyes narrowed. "I want to protect you, not control you."

Violet smiled, then set her hand atop his fingers where they rested on his thigh.

He turned his palm over, gently twining his fingers with hers. "Honestly, I can do a better job looking after you if you're with me anyway, and this should be a quick meeting. No danger included. I was probably overreacting. Seeing danger where there isn't any. I think my run-in with Mr. Masterson earlier has me spooked."

"Well, hopefully Santos has something good, and this will be over by morning." Gratitude swelled in Violet's chest. She was glad for Santos's help. Thankful her grandma was finally awake and that there was security stationed right outside her room. Thankful also for not one but two of Fortress Security's finest looking after Maggie and her. Things were definitely looking up.

She scanned the peaceful night, enjoying the moment until something caught her eye in the mirror. Violet tensed at the distant glow of emergency flashers and her stomach knotted.

"Fire truck," Wyatt said, a smile curving his lips. "For a minute I thought I was being pulled over again." He eased onto the berm so the bleating truck could blow past. A moment later, Wyatt repeated the maneuver to allow an ambulance the space it needed on the narrow road.

"That's not good," Violet said, attention glued to the flashers disappearing up ahead. "Wyatt?"

Wyatt swore. He'd seen it, too.

"They're going toward Grandma's house."

Wyatt pressed the gas pedal. Hard.

Violet's head clung to the seat. Her muscles clenched. Her chest pinched. "What if something has happened to Sawyer?"

Wyatt tossed his cell phone from the cup holder. "Call."

Violet scrolled through his contacts and hit Call. The phone rang slowly, time ticking at half pace while she waited. "Voice mail."

Wyatt's grip tightened on the wheel. "Sawyer's good. No one could've gotten the jump on him."

Sure, Violet thought. *He also has a quick temper and obvious PTSD.* An assailant didn't need to surprise him as much as provoke him, and she imagined the sheriff would see any response of Sawyer's as justification for firing his weapon.

A pair of deputy cruisers appeared up ahead, coming at them from the opposite direction, sirens on and flashers illuminating the sky. They, too, took hasty turns in the direction of Grandma's house.

"Holy," Wyatt whispered as the flames came into view.

Violet's gut gave a mighty heave.

The smoke was black and thick. The flames cut through the starry sky. Grandma's driveway and the street out front were clogged with emergency vehicles and officials in a multitude of uniforms. Firefighters were posted on the lawn, directing water from great white hoses. EMTs waited by ambulances. Deputies stared openmouthed at the shooting flames.

Violet sat motionless in her seat, horrified and sickened at the sight of her childhood home going up in flames. All the mementos that she'd so carefully packed for tomorrow's move. Gone. The kitchen where she learned to cook. The bedroom where Grandpa read her stories and tucked her in at night. Everything she knew about her mom, wherever she was. Gone. Gone. Gone.

Wyatt opened her door and pulled her out with a hug. His trademark Stetson was low over his eyes. "I'm sorry about the house, but I sure am glad no one was here."

Violet nodded woodenly. The acrid scent of smoke stung her eyes and burned her throat. Heat from the inferno blew in waves over her skin. "I'm going to try Sawyer again."

Wyatt went around to collect Maggie. He returned a moment later.

"Voice mail," she said once more.

Wyatt moved toward the nearest ambulance. "Maybe an EMT will fill us in."

Violet followed, praying silently for Sawyer's safety.

Then the unmistakable outline of his Jeep came into view, parked between emergency vehicles. "Wyatt," she whispered.

Wyatt swore under his breath. He straightened his hat, then passed Maggie to Violet. "Hey!" he called, jogging closer to the home.

A nearby fireman turned in his direction. "I think there's someone in the house."

The man started at the sight of Wyatt with Violet on his heels. "You need to get back, sir, ma'am. Maintain a clear distance. It's not safe."

Wyatt bristled. "I think my buddy's in there. His Jeep's in the drive."

The fireman shook his head. "Structure's not sound. We haven't found anyone inside, and I'm pulling my men out."

The sharp cry of a siren turned the little crowd toward the road.

The sheriff's cruiser rocked to a stop in the center of the road. He moved solemnly on foot in their direction. His flat expression rattled Violet's nerves. He didn't care that her family home was on fire. Didn't even look surprised. "I'm afraid you two need to step away from the home and let these men work."

Wyatt stalked toward him. "What have you done?"

An upstairs window shattered, and Wyatt spun in the direction of the sound. "What was that?" He looked briefly at Violet with hope in his eyes.

What if Sawyer was trying to get out? She'd thought so, too.

Wyatt scanned the scene, then burst into a run, disappearing into the smoke.

"No!" Violet screamed. "Wyatt!"

Maggie cried and bucked in her mother's arms.

"Shhh. Sorry. Sorry." Violet bounced gently, rocking and cooing to the baby as she moved slowly back from the raging heat. "Do something," she demanded of the sheriff and fireman, both staring blankly at Wyatt's silhouette as he vanished into the smoke engulfing the land around her home.

The fireman smashed the button on his walkie-talkie. "We've got a man heading into the building at the east first-floor entrance."

Static crackled back.

Violet's stomach knotted. Maggie's continued cries shredded her mama's heart into pieces. "Shh. Shh. Shh." She tried unsuccessfully and wished she could cry, too.

"Captain," a male voice rattled through the line. "House is empty. We're heading out back. See if we can save the barn."

The fireman gave Violet and Maggie a long, regretful look. He depressed the walkie-talkie button once more. "Watch for the civilian on your way out."

Violet closed her eyes and sent up desperate prayers for both Wyatt and Sawyer.

"Ma'am," the fireman said, forcing Violet's eyes open once more. "He might've gone around back. Maybe he saw something we didn't. My men are headed there now. We'll know soon enough."

Violet nodded, wiping tears on her wrist. Seeing what others didn't see was kind of Wyatt's shtick.

She stepped back farther, contemplating a seat in Wyatt's truck, away from the drifting smoke, when a gunshot rang out. "What was that?"

The sheriff's face turned in the direction of the sound, but he made no move to acknowledge it.

"Hey!" Violet yelled over the crackling fire, rushing water and endless chatter of a dozen emergency responders gathered on the lawn.

He pointedly ignored her, looking instead at the other stupefied faces around them.

"Was that a gunshot?" the fireman asked.

The sheriff shook his head. Negative.

"Liar!" Violet shoved the sheriff with days' worth of anger. "Do something!"

The sheriff stumbled back, caught off guard by her outburst. "It was probably the snap of burning wood."

The fireman wrinkled his brow. "Sounded like gunfire."

"Ammo in heat," the sheriff said.

Violet felt the tears come again as she stared into the thick smoke, watching each returning fireman arrive empty-handed. No casualties. No Sawyer. No Wyatt.

"Fire's out," an emerging man explained. His hair was gray, and his helmet was tucked beneath his arm. "Circle up."

The fire crew moved toward him, away from the home and closer to their truck, turning their backs on her and Sheriff Masterson.

Violet listened while they made plans to minimize the damage from the home's inevitable collapse.

The deputies tipped their hats before climbing back into their cruisers.

The EMTs packed up and rolled out.

Violet watched the smoke.

An eternity later, a silhouette appeared in the haze, wearing the cowboy hat she knew so well.

Violet moved toward Wyatt, drawn like a magnet.

She took a wide path in his direction, steering clear of the firefighters in their huddle and slowing when the rear corner of her grandma's house came clearly into view. She avoided the thickest smoke, angling past a patch of shrubs and trees in the side yard, hyper-aware of Maggie on her hip and the reaching tendrils of smoke as it slithered over the ground.

When the figure grew clearer, a handgun became visible in his grip.

The fine hairs on her arms and neck rose to attention. Something was off in his stance, the tilt of his head, the sinister feel in the air. Violet pulled to a stop.

The figure advanced, removing itself from the shadows. *Mr. Masterson.* She took several steps back, keeping a distance between them.

Her toe caught on something.

Someone groaned.

"Wyatt?" She dropped beside the man at her feet. "Oh my goodness! What happened? Are you okay?" Masterson's gun flashed back into mind.

Blood soaked the side of Wyatt's shirt and seeped low into his waistband. She *had* heard a gunshot earlier.

"You shot him," she cried.

Wyatt's eyes fluttered open and rolled. "Go," he croaked. "Run!"

Violet jerked upright. *Run.* Get help. "Okay." She turned for the fire truck just beyond the patch of trees.

"Ah ah ah." The silhouette with the gun stepped into clear view, Wyatt's Stetson perched on his head. "Time to go," the former sheriff told her, rearranging Wyatt's hat on his head.

Violet stumbled back. "No. I'm not leaving him."

He pointed the gun at Violet. "Are you sure? Because I won't ask again."

Sickness coiled in her gut. Would he really shoot her? Holding a baby? She turned in search of help. The fire truck blocked her view of the firefighters. "I'll scream," she threatened.

"Scream and I finish him off right now. How about that?" He lowered the barrel to Wyatt's head and pressed it hard to his skin, rocking Wyatt's forehead back.

Wyatt tried to roll onto his stomach, tried to push onto his knees despite the blood pooling everywhere. He made a swipe for Masterson's feet, but he smoothly stepped aside.

"Ma'am?" a male voice called, presumably the fireman she'd spoken to earlier. "You back here? Everything all right?"

Mr. Masterson cocked the gun.

"I'll go," she whispered, then followed the direction of Masterson's gun to a side-by-side vehicle parked in the trees a few feet away.

Violet cuddled Maggie to her chest as the off-road vehicle gunned to life. At least the fireman looking for her would find Wyatt now. At least he still had a chance.

Chapter Nineteen

Wyatt dragged himself onto his knees and forearms, coughing and wincing with each pull and tug of his wound. He'd been shot before, but the pain of seeing Violet and Maggie forced into Masterson's hands was worse than anything he'd ever known.

"Help!" a fireman called, racing to Wyatt's side. "Help!" The man snapped into action, immediately evaluating his injuries and rousing assistance from his team.

Wyatt listened as they spoke in familiar acronyms and medical terms. His vitals were good. His heart rate was high, but what did they expect? He'd been shot and seen the woman he loved abducted along with the baby who'd stolen his heart.

"It's a through-and-through, but you're going to need an ambulance," the man said. "What happened?"

Wyatt gritted his teeth against the pain. "Masterson shot me."

Wyatt had seen someone in the haze of smoke and raced to get his hands on the guy. He'd hoped it was Sawyer, but would've settled for capturing the arsonist. A gunshot had stopped him short and planted him in the grass where he'd blacked out until Violet tripped over him.

Anger pooled in his core as he recalled the way Masterson had spoken to Violet, the way he'd grabbed her and forced her away.

"The ambulance is on the way," someone said. "It hadn't gotten far, and they're turning back now."

"Call Deputy Santos," Wyatt said. "I don't need an ambulance. I need to get to Masterson before he kills them." He fumbled his phone from his pocket and dialed Santos himself. "Stitch me, so I can go."

"Santos," the deputy answered on the first ring.

"He's got the girls," Wyatt said, his head light from pain and blood loss. "Meet me at the well."

"We're already on it," Santos said. "I've got your man with me. We're changing direction now. Give us twenty minutes."

Wyatt disconnected with a prayer. He hoped to hell the old man was headed to the well with Violet and Maggie. Wyatt wasn't sure where else to look for him, and every second mattered.

The hands of the fireman cleaning his wound stilled. His face wrinkled in confusion. "Who did you say might kill them?"

"Masterson," Wyatt groaned. "The sheriff's dad."

The man scanned the area. "The sheriff was just here. Where'd he go?"

"Probably after his dad." Wyatt shot a pleading look to the man with gloved hands on his side. "If you give me the suture kit, I'll do it myself."

The man opened the kit with a frown. "The ambulance is only a few minutes away. I haven't done this in twenty years, and that was in the field in Fallujah. The scar I left behind was monstrous."

"Did your patient live?" Wyatt asked.

The man's face twisted into a proud smile. "Yes, sir."

Wyatt gave a stiff dip of his chin. "Get started."

VIOLET DRAGGED HER FEET as Mr. Masterson shoved her forward through the trees toward the old well where she'd nearly been killed not long ago. Her muscles were rigid with fear as he forced her along. Terror clenched her heart and stole her breath with each and every footfall. "You don't have to do this," she pleaded as the barbed wire perimeter came into view. Chunks of earth were tossed and scattered where the explosion had occurred. Her tongue swelled and her mouth dried. "I won't say anything to anyone. I swear it."

"Shut up," he said. "Keep moving."

Violet's chest constricted and burned. "I know that what you did was an accident," she croaked. "You were young and scared. You panicked. Anyone would have done what you did in that situation."

Masterson hoisted the barbed wire for her to duck underneath. "Would you?"

Violet bit her lip, unable to take another step. Sheer panic stopped her pitiful momentum. She couldn't cross that line, and the lie Masterson wanted to hear just wouldn't come. She wouldn't have done what he did. She would have gotten Henry Davis help, or at least tried. She would have carried her accidental victim in her arms if needed to try to save his life. She would have confessed everything and prayed for forgiveness.

Yes, accidents happen, but what Masterson had done wasn't an accident. Maybe when Henry Davis fell and hit his head, but not after Masterson threw him down a well. Not after he hid the lie for fifty years. He'd watched while Henry Davis's family searched for him. He'd let the reporters call him a deserter. Masterson had even sworn his own wife to silence, isolated her so she had no one to tell.

No. Violet wouldn't have done what Masterson had done.

"That's what I thought," he said. "Now duck under this wire, or I'll take your baby and let her crawl around again, test her luck on my minefield."

Violet tightened her hold on Maggie. "You're the one who put her outside the library. You left her alone. She could've gotten into the street. She could have been killed!"

"That was the idea," he said, waving the gun at her baby until Violet ducked under the wire as he'd commanded. "With a tragedy like that in play, you would've lost all interest in digging up my secret. But, oh no, you just keep coming." He cocked the pistol and pointed it at Maggie. "Hurry up. Get over here or I shoot."

Violet turned her hip away from him, putting as much distance as possible between the psychopath and her baby. The well was covered in shadows, and she had no intention of going one step closer. "Please. Just let us go. She can't testify against you, and I won't. For her sake."

Masterson blinked as headlights flashed through the night, bouncing across Potter's Field and illuminating the abandoned well. Violet's stomach twisted at the sight. The plywood covering had been dragged away. Masterson had prepared for this. He wouldn't stop until she and Maggie were down there with Henry Davis.

Mr. Masterson grimaced at the open well. "What the hell?"

Sheriff Masterson appeared in the flood of light, breezing through the field in their direction. "Dad!" The sheriff ducked under the barbed wire and stepped carefully in his father's direction. "You're out of control. You burned that woman's house down."

Mr. Masterson turned a feral expression on his son. "Get back, Junior. I did what I had to do, just like I always have. You don't need to be a part of this."

"I'm the sheriff," he screamed. "Of course I'm a part of this. And you need to stop." He rested a palm on his sidearm, eyes wide, bewildered and crazed. "I can't let you do this. Not again."

Violet took a tiny step back. She positioned Maggie against her chest and secured her in a bear hug, preparing to run.

"No, you don't." Mr. Masterson's hand snapped out and caught her by the arm. "Let's go."

Violet jerked away from his grip. Stumbling for footing, she tripped over herself and fell heavily onto her backside. A barb from the fence ripped through the tender skin of her side. Maggie wailed as they thudded against the ground.

Violet clutched her baby to her chest. "Please don't do this."

The sheriff stepped forward, gun in hand. "Dad." There was warning in his eyes.

Masterson yanked Violet onto her feet and gripped her to his side. "I've told you to butt out. You'd be wise to listen. Your hands are clean."

"Hardly." Wyatt's voice was salve to Violet's frantic heart. He stepped into view behind the sheriff, a gun in one hand, the other palm pressed against his bloody side. "Put the gun down, Masterson. Let her go."

The sheriff made a disgusted sound and turned on Wyatt. "Get over there with them before I toss you down the well myself. This is family business."

Wyatt sidestepped the sheriff, unfazed by the threat and splitting his attention between the armed men. "We know what you've both done," he said. "It took fifty years, but the truth has caught up with you."

Mr. Masterson scoffed. He looked at his son. "Put these three down, and it's over. That's all we've got to do."

"No." Wyatt shook his head. "Not at all. You see, your wife told Violet's grandma everything. She found out the story was true and called my private security firm for protection while she turned you both in. She's awake now. She told us the story. My man's been down your well." He nodded toward the yawning hole only a few feet from Violet and freshly uncovered.

Wyatt eased through the headlights, stepping carefully into position near the line of trees, forming the third tip of a small triangle with the Mastersons. "We know Henry Davis's body is in that well. We know you bought the property to protect your secret. You drove the demolition derby car used to run Violet off the road and visited the Ames home to vandalize our vehicles." He swung his eyes to the younger man. "We know you broke into Mrs. Ames's home after one of you tried to kill her. You left a threatening note for Violet at the hospital. Reported my truck as stolen. And your father set that fire tonight."

The Mastersons exchanged heated glares.

Wyatt's steady tone was at odds with his pale skin. Beads of sweat gathered along his forehead and at his temples. "Now you're going to pay for your crimes."

Mr. Masterson dug his fingers deep into Violet's hair and forced her forward, bent face-first over the gaping well. "I don't think so."

Maggie wailed and clung to her mother's chest above the seemingly endless black hole.

"Stop!" Violet cried. "Please. No."

Behind her, a gun went off, and the fingers in her hair loosened.

Mr. Masterson released her with a jolt, nearly toppling her into the open well. He dived at his son in a rage. "You took a shot at me?"

Violet fell against the well's brick edges, landing hard on one hip before scurrying back from the hole. She stopped short as the land mines returned to mind, and she sobbed against her sweet baby's crying face, curving her shoulders over Maggie where they sat on the treacherous earth.

Before them, Wyatt wrestled with the sheriff, both angling for a dropped sidearm, presumably the one that had gone off moments before.

Mr. Masterson stalked toward them, gaze intent on the dark ground. His boot connected with Wyatt's blood-soaked side and sent him rolling across the grass.

Violet winced at the sight of the gruesome connection. She pressed Maggie tighter to her chest, using her hands to shield her baby's eyes from all the ugly sights.

Wyatt was on his knees in a second, face red and fists curled. He jolted forward, connecting his shoulder to the old man's middle, the way he had saved Violet's life earlier. Mr. Masterson grunted as the air whooshed from his lungs, and he landed with a hard thud and a desperate groan.

The sheriff flew at Wyatt, but was deflected with a well-aimed punch to the gut. Sheriff Masterson doubled over in pain and was rewarded with Wyatt's elbow against his neck and shoulder.

Wyatt twisted the sheriff's hands behind his back and used his cuffs against him.

Mr. Masterson creaked into a sit, rasping in pain. "You can't win," he said. "That man is the sheriff. No one will believe you, and the buck stops with him." He raked his hand over the dark ground in search of his fallen pistol, then pointed it at Wyatt.

A new set of headlights flooded the scene. The vehicle rocked to a stop several yards away, while the faint wails of emergency vehicles whirred to life some-where in the distance.

Violet watched in confusion as a coroner's van pulled in and took its place beside the sheriff's car. A deputy's cruiser and two ambulances followed.

Mr. Masterson lowered the weapon.

"Hello, Sheriff Masterson." Deputy Santos's voice flowed from a backlit figure moving through the blind-ing headlights. "Wyatt, Miss Ames, I'd like you to meet Sam Culley, Grove County coroner."

Sawyer appeared in the light, having climbed down from the passenger's side of the coroner's van. The incoming trio stopped at the edge of the barbed wire perimeter, clear of the mines.

"About time," Wyatt groaned, shoving off the sher-iff's back. He dusted his palms and nudged the cuffed sheriff with the toe of one boot. "Did you know that in the great state of Kentucky, only the sitting coroner can arrest the sheriff?" he asked. He turned a cheery smile on Mr. Masterson. "Turns out the buck doesn't stop here."

Deputy Santos shined a heavy flashlight on the ground, stepping carefully toward Mr. Masterson to relieve him of his weapon.

Sawyer skulked toward Wyatt, gaze fixed on the ground. "You think I'm slow, but I had to go get this guy out of bed." He motioned to the coroner, now reading the sheriff his rights from the safety of the perimeter fence. "He doesn't even live in this town. And we followed Santos over here, who drives like my great-grandmother."

Santos shot him a look. "Shut up."

Wyatt shook Sawyer's hand in one strong pump.

He snatched his Stetson off the old man's head, then headed straight for Violet's side.

Violet's sobs were stifled for Maggie's sake, and her heart was fit to explode. The incredible rush of relief and anticipation of being in Wyatt's arms once more was nearly painful.

"Are you okay?" Wyatt hoisted her up with one arm and took Maggie from her with the other. He cuddled them both to his chest. "I thought I'd be too late."

Maggie snuggled instantly against him. Her cries had faded to grateful whimpers.

Violet knew exactly how her daughter felt. In Wyatt's arms, everything was okay and anything was possible.

VIOLET AND WYATT sat in the stiff chairs of the hospital waiting room while Maggie toddled speedily across the floor. It was hard to believe that nearly a year had passed since Violet had gotten that terrifying call. The one that told her Grandma was in a coma. The one that had changed her life in every possible way.

"How are you doing?" Wyatt asked, concerned as always about Violet's comfort, well-being, ability to rest and every general whim.

"Perfect," she said, feeling the depth of truth in the word.

Wyatt grinned. "Good." He pulled Maggie onto his lap as she stumbled against his legs in a windmill of chubby arms and giggles.

Grandma cruised through the doorway a moment

later, an expert on her cane. The months of physical therapy following her accident had left her in better condition than she'd started, and the overall experience had given her a new lease on life. She didn't even mind the cane. "Am I late?"

Wyatt and Maggie greeted her with hugs and cheek kisses. "Nope."

"Excellent." She took a seat at Violet's side and patted her arm. "I've got things all set at home. All I need now is your little miss."

Wyatt raised Maggie in the air. "Here she comes," he said, flying his sweet girl like an airplane to her great-grandmother's lap.

Grandma kissed Maggie's nose, then raised her eyes to the soldier who'd saved all their lives. "Trial's over. Did you hear?"

Wyatt nodded. "We did. The prosecuting attorney called after breakfast."

"He called me, too," Grandma said, looking pensive but satisfied.

Violet tried to smile, but she had too many mixed emotions to manage it.

According to the attorney, Mr. Masterson was found guilty for the murders of Henry Davis and Ruth, for the attempted murder of Grandma and Wyatt, the abduction and attempted murders of Violet, Maggie and his wife who fell from Grandma's barn but later died from complications of her already diminished condition. Along with about a dozen other things. Sheriff Masterson was found guilty for his role and participation in the extensive cover-up and everything that had involved.

It was hard to be happy about the verdict, even with justice served, when so many people had lost their lives.

"Mrs. Stone?" A nurse called from the waiting room door, her eyes settling quickly on Violet.

Warmth rushed through her, as it always did at the sound of her name with Wyatt's. There really wasn't anything greater than being loved by him. And to think she'd tried to swear off military men.

He was on his feet in an instant, reaching for her. He hoisted Violet easily onto her very swollen feet and smiled. "Beautiful."

She rolled her eyes and rubbed the base of her aching back. She'd gained thirty-six pounds and was shaped like a whale, but he never stopped insisting she was perfect.

She slipped her hand into his and shook her head at the man who'd saved her life in every way possible. Her handsome, courageous, honorable husband. "I love you."

He leaned down to kiss her, and her knees nearly buckled with pleasure. As usual.

Grandma clapped her hands together. "That's our cue, Miss Maggie." She set Maggie on her feet, stood and took her hand. "We'll meet you at my place for lunch and the big news," she told Violet and Wyatt. "Your family was already starting to arrive when I left."

Grandma's place was now just down the street from

Violet, Wyatt and Maggie. Grandma had collected the insurance money from the fire, sold her land and gotten a cottage in Lexington while she finished recovering from last year's fall. The cottage was warm and inviting with less upkeep and maintenance than the farm had required. More time for things that mattered, like family, she'd said as she signed the papers. She'd even planted a rose garden in the backyard.

Wyatt and Violet kissed Maggie and Grandma goodbye, then followed the nurse to an ultrasound room.

"Have you decided?" the nurse asked. "Would you like to know the gender of your baby?"

Violet smiled up at her husband. "Absolutely."

The whole family was gathering for that news as they spoke, and Violet couldn't wait to start her next adventure with the man she knew would never let her go.

* * * * *

Don't miss the next book in Julie Anne Lindsey's
Fortress Defense miniseries,
Missing in the Mountains,
available next month!

YOU HAVE JUST READ A HARLEQUIN® INTRIGUE® BOOK

If you were **captivated** by the **gripping, page-turning romantic suspense,** be sure to look for all six Harlequin® Intrigue® books every month.

AVAILABLE THIS MONTH FROM
Harlequin Intrigue®

A THREAT TO HIS FAMILY
Longview Ridge Ranch • by Delores Fossen

When threatened by an unknown assailant, single dad Deputy Owen Slater must protect his daughter with the help of PI Laney Martin, who is investigating her sister's murder. Can they find out who is after them before someone else is killed?

TACTICAL FORCE
Declan's Defenders • by Elle James

Former marine and Declan's Defenders member Jack Snow and White House staffer Anne Bellamy must work together to stop an assassin from killing the president of the United States. But when their search makes Anne the killer's target, can they track down the criminal before he finds them?

CODE CONSPIRACY
Red, White and Built: Delta Force Deliverance
by Carol Ericson

When Gray Prescott's Delta Force commander goes AWOL under suspicious circumstances, he turns to his ex, computer hacker extraordinaire Jerrica West, for answers. But what they find might be deadly...

DEADLY COVER-UP
Fortress Defense • by Julie Anne Lindsey

With the help of bodyguard Wyatt Stone, newly single mother Violet Ames races to discover the truth about her grandmother's near-fatal accident. Before long, she'll learn that incident is part of a conspiracy long protected by a powerful local family.

BRACE FOR IMPACT
by Janice Kay Johnson

Maddy Kane is a key witness in a high-profile murder case, and her only chance at survival lies in the hands of former army medic Will Gannon. With armed goons hot on their trail, can they survive long enough for Maddy to testify?

IN HIS SIGHTS
Stealth • by Danica Winters

Jarrod Martin's investigation into a crime syndicate takes an unexpected turn when he joins forces with criminal heiress Mindy Kohl to protect her five-year-old niece from ruthless killers.

_____

LOOK FOR THESE AND OTHER HARLEQUIN INTRIGUE BOOKS WHEREVER BOOKS ARE SOLD, INCLUDING MOST BOOKSTORES, SUPERMARKETS, DISCOUNT STORES AND DRUGSTORES.

HIATMBPA0120

Love Harlequin romance?

DISCOVER.

Be the first to find out about promotions, news and exclusive content!

Facebook.com/HarlequinBooks

Twitter.com/HarlequinBooks

Instagram.com/HarlequinBooks

Pinterest.com/HarlequinBooks

ReaderService.com

EXPLORE.

Sign up for the Harlequin e-newsletter and download a free book from any series at **TryHarlequin.com.**

CONNECT.

Join our Harlequin community to share your thoughts and connect with other romance readers!
Facebook.com/groups/HarlequinConnection

HARLEQUIN®

**ROMANCE WHEN
YOU NEED IT**